总序

名著金库

永恒经典

柔波集

集校版全集

Rubaiyat of Omar Khayyarm

第1版、第2版、第3版、第4版、第5版

[波斯] 奥马尔·哈亚姆 著
[英] 爱德华·菲茨杰拉德 英译
文爱艺 译

目次

总序

文爱艺

文学史上，因一本薄薄的小册子而永垂不朽的并不鲜见，然出自地域相距万里之遥、时空相隔700年之久的合作，却绝无仅有——这就是拿在你手中的这部《柔波集》（*Rubáiyát*）。

《柔波集》是奥马尔·哈亚姆的四行诗集。

《柔波集》原名*Rubáiyát*，是柔波Rubái的复数，柔波也译作“鲁拜”“柔巴依”。柔波（Rubái）源自阿拉伯语，在古波斯又称为“Taraneh”，意为“四行”、“四行诗”或“绝句”，是维吾尔族古典抒情诗的形式之一。原是古波斯和塔吉克的民间口头创作，后与由突厥文明传入波斯的唐代绝句相融合，经波斯诗歌之父鲁达基（Rudagi, 858—941）之手定型而形成的新诗体。

这种古典抒情诗的基本特征是：每首四行，既可独立成篇，又可循环相连。每行由五个音组构成，要求第一、二、四行押韵，第三行一般不押韵。它形式完美、结构典雅、格律严谨，有鲜明的节奏，适于吟咏；诗体类似我国的“绝句”。内容多是描述生命如寄、盛衰无常的遭际，以及及时行乐、纵酒放歌的人生追求。

奥马尔·哈亚姆有“波斯李白”之称，在纵酒狂歌的表象之下，他洞彻生命的虚幻无常，以绝美的诗，将人生的悲哀表达得淋漓尽致。

奥马尔·哈亚姆的诗风深情、豪迈、旷

达，诗作融科学家的观照与诗人的灵感于一体，成为文学艺术上的辉煌杰作。

奥马尔·哈亚姆的诗大部分有关死亡与享乐，用了很多笔墨来讽刺来世以及神，这与当时的世俗风尚相去甚远。

《柔波集》其实是一些零散的笔记，哈亚姆死后，由他的学生整理出来。19世纪，英国作家爱德华·菲茨杰拉德（Edward Fitzgerald）将《柔波集》译成英文。因其译文精美，从此《柔波集》不再只是历史笔记，而成为著名诗集被世界所接受。

一

奥马尔·哈亚姆（波斯文：عمر خیام，拉丁文：Omar Khayyám，英文：Omar Khayyam，全名：Ghiyáth al-Din Abul Fateh Omar Ibn Ibráhim al-khayyám，又有莪默·伽亚谟、奥马开俨、欧玛尔·海亚姆、奥玛珈音等译名，1048年5月18日—1122年12月4日），波斯诗人、哲学家、天文学家、数学家、历史学家、法学家、医学家。他一生研究各门学问，尤精天文学，当时的苏丹非常器重哈亚姆，委以修订历法的重任。1079年实行的新历亚拉里历比蒋牟西旧历更为精确。

哈亚姆是当时著名的数学家，1070年写下影响深远的《代数问题的论证》（*Treatise on Demonstration of Problems of Algebra*）。书中阐释了代数的原理，令波斯数学传至欧洲。他发现解决三次方程，以及更高次方程的方法。除诸多天文图谱以及一部代数学论文之外，哈亚姆还留下了诗集《柔波集》（又译《鲁拜集》《柔巴依集》）。

其姓哈亚姆（Khayyám）意为“帐篷制作者”，由此推断他生于手工家庭。他曾用诗句表述由此生发的感慨：

Khayyám, who stitched the tents of science,
Has fallen in grief's furnace and been suddenly burned;
The shears of Fate have cut the tent ropes of his life,
And the broker of Hope has sold him for nothing!

哈亚姆，他曾缝制科学的帐篷，
如今落入痛苦的炉中，被深深地灼伤；
命运之刀砍断了他生存之篷的绳索，
希望这个骗子又将他出卖！

他大约1048年生于呼拉商州（Khorassán）内沙布尔（Naishápúr，现位于伊朗东部），该地为亚细亚大陆所拥抱；气候温和，土地丰美，适于农业，尤其棉花的栽培最为繁盛，使得棉织品、绢、呢自古驰名；盛产突厥玉、宝石；在当时是波斯文化的中心，历史上曾是波斯首府。

他是一名什叶派的穆斯林，小时候曾在巴尔赫（今阿富汗北部）居住，并跟随谢赫（意为“教长”）穆罕默德·曼苏尔（Muhammad

Mansuri）学习。其后，跟随当时最为有名的伊玛姆 · 穆瓦法克（lmán Mowaffak，旧译“野芒”，又译“摩瓦伐克”）学习。

据载，诗人幼年在故乡与学友尼扎姆·乌尔·莫尔克（Nizám ul Mulk）、哈桑·本·萨巴赫（Hasan Ben Sabbáh）曾就学于著名学者伊玛姆 · 穆瓦法克（lmán Mowaffak）。一日，三人相聚，哈桑说道：“世人都说做穆瓦法克的弟子会得到幸福，假若不能获得幸福怎么办？”莫尔克和哈亚姆答道：“怎么都行。”哈桑提议：“那我们立誓，日后有福同享。”之后，莫尔克官至宰相，举荐哈桑做了官。但哈桑嫌升迁太慢，阴谋取代莫尔克，失败后遭贬，结果沦为伊斯玛仪派（lsmailians）——一个暗杀集团的首领，并杀死了莫尔克。于是，哈桑·本·萨巴赫成为历史上最恐怖的一个名字。

诗人阿塔尔记录莫尔克被杀时吟叹哈亚姆诗中的句子：

神啊，我正在风的手中消逝

哈亚姆拒绝官场的诱惑，不要官职，只向莫尔克要求道：“你可给予我的最大恩惠，就是让我在你财富庇护的一角安静地生活，去广泛传播科学的优异，且为你的健康和富足祈祷。”于是莫尔克便从国库中每年赠予他1200密（Mithkál）的年金，并赐予他皇宫旁的一处居所。之后，他在家乡一直忙于各种知识的探求，投身于天文学、数学的著述，并参与了日历的革新，是当时天文学、数学的权威。此外，他博学多才，撰写了很多有关哲学、历史、法学和医学的论文。

莫尔克死后，由于国家动乱，他的生活陷入困境，贫病交加，于1123年在家乡抑郁而逝。他留在人间的最后一句话是："真主啊！我在力所能及的范围努力了解你；请原谅，我了解你是我靠拢你的唯一手段。"

很多学者质疑这个故事的真实性，因为哈亚姆与尼札姆·穆尔克的年纪相差30岁，两人不太可能一起上学，但这个故事广为流传，这可能是由于三人的卓越表现：哈亚姆代表科学方面的成就；哈桑·本·萨巴赫代表变革；尼扎姆·乌尔·莫尔克代表权力、秩序和法治。

他的学生赫瓦加·尼扎米（Khwájah Nizámi）记载："有一天他对我说：'每年两次北风会把花儿带来，覆盖我的墓地。'他的话令我惊奇，但我知道这绝非戏言，因为他从不说虚话。若干年后，约1136年，我偶然重访内沙布尔，在一个星期五的黄昏，来到他的长眠之地。哦，看哪！他的墓地恰好在一个花园的外面，果树把结满累累果实的枝丫伸出墙来，把花撒满墓地，连墓碑也埋在落花之中。"赫瓦加·尼扎米想起奥马尔·哈亚姆说过的话，掩面哭泣。

这位多才多艺的奇才，在自由自在的学术生涯中，忙里偷闲随手用柔波（Rubái）的形式记录了数百条充溢着音韵之美的思想。然而，这些思想，当时在他的国度却从来没有真正流行过，尽管现在《柔波集》已成为波斯文学繁盛的标志，并且淹没了哈亚姆在天文、数学、历史、法学、医学等诸领域所取得的盛名。

他的这些思想，与当时盛行的神秘主义传统大异其趣。在所处的中世纪，他是一个彻底的现世论者，有着不羁的独立个性和强烈的离经叛道色彩，极力彰显摆脱神或君王之类所谓超凡者的精神控制。他根本不关心来世，说："我就是地狱和天堂。"

他成功地运用柔波（Rubái）这种艺术形式，表述了他对生活、社会、宗教、哲学等方面的见解，并且善于从日常生活中选取常见的形象，来传达对社会的认识或哲学的思考。他的诗既充满叛逆精神，又洋溢着对生活的热爱，否定来世，以此向禁欲主义提出挑战；既谴责社会制度的黑暗，鞭笞伪善，又抒发了对自由平等的向往；既有对现实的无情解剖，又认定世界是美丽可爱的；既充满浓郁的哲学意蕴，又歌颂了生活的芬芳情趣。然而，他毕竟生活在宗教占主导地位的国度，因此形成了他颇为矛盾的世界观。在一些诗中，他也表述了带有宿命论和不可知论的观点，并流露出及时行乐等消极情绪。

但这些都无损于诗篇本身的优美：形象鲜明生动、语言朴素动听、韵律委婉灵变、情感强烈真挚的诗句，穿过时空，终于征服了远隔万水千山的英国著名学者、作家、翻译家、诗人爱德华·菲茨杰拉德（Edward Fitzgerald，1809—1883），从而在它诞生700余年之后，重放异彩，获得世界性的声誉，其版本之多、流传之广、引用之众，仅次于《圣经》。

爱德华·菲茨杰拉德（Edward Fitzgerald）英译的《柔波集》（*Rubáiyát*）《奥马尔·哈亚姆之—柔波集》（*RUBAIYAT OF OMAR KHAYYAM*），1859年匿名出版发表，共101首，404行。起先无人问津，后被文豪发现推荐，从此微烛挑明而光芒四射，奇迹般地蜚声西方各国，轰动世界文坛。

这些成就的取得，并非一帆风顺。

二

爱德华·菲茨杰拉德于1809年3月31日生于英国萨福克郡（Suffolk）布瑞费尔德村（Bredfield）的一个富商之家，其资产包括著名的内兹比（Naseby）战场的地产。他受到良好的贵族式教育，曾就学于剑桥大学三一学院。他继承了大笔遗产，使得他无需从事任何职业，就能过着衣食无忧的高雅生活，从而自如地研究文学和艺术。他生性恬静，大学毕业后住在乡下一栋舒适的别墅里，深居简出，过着退隐般的安逸生活，成了一位安安静静的文学爱好者。

他喜欢交友、爱好音乐、划船、种花；丁尼生（Tennyson）、萨克雷（Thackeray）、汤普森（W.H.Thompson）等文学巨匠都是他的好友。他们对他的人品和学识给予很高的评价。他不仅拥有丰富的学识，而且具有惊人的鉴赏力。1851

年，即他42岁那年，出版了他的第一本书，一部拟古对话集，并翻译了一些希腊和西班牙的文学作品，之后，又销声匿迹。

1853年他44岁时，跟友人考威尔（Edward Cowell）开始研究波斯，很快掌握并熟练地运用波斯语。无意间，他接触到奥马尔·哈亚姆不为人知的《柔波集》遗稿，很快迷上了它。这些丽词佳句，充满思辨色彩的奇异诗章，满足了他逃离污浊尘世、沉溺于梦幻的心境。此外，他深信波斯的哈亚姆和自己的爱尔兰先祖之间存在着某种联系，他甚至觉得自己就是那位被遗忘的波斯诗人。因此，他视哈亚姆的《柔波集》如自己的生命，在译成英文的过程中，殚精竭虑，倾注了所有心血。

开始，他试着把这些优美的诗篇译成拉丁文。之后，他放弃了这一尝试，而是直接把它译成英文。有趣的是，在他逝世10年后，有人把他的这些英文转译成拉丁文。

爱德华·菲茨杰拉德的“翻译”属于大刀阔斧、天马行空般的“意译”，借奥马尔·哈亚姆的灵感重新创作，酝酿出辞藻优美的诗章，将几百首原作排列组合整理，如珍珠删串合连成了最终的101首，“创作”的成分甚多。但是他保持了原诗的诗意、格律、韵味，译文仍具有浓烈的东方色彩。

经过 6 年多的艰辛劳作，他把这些令人喜爱的四行诗译成英文，并按照自己的体验重新编排，使它成为一部有头有尾、肌体完整的有趣诗集。打开诗集，你首先感到旭日初升，哈亚姆一边喝着美酒，一边发表种种议论，随着时间的流逝，他对上苍的不公越来越感到愤慨，对人世的炎凉越来越感到失望……

这种巧妙的安排，使原来毫无关联的诗章，在时间上有了一种连续性，在内容上有一种内在的逻辑性，使得整部诗集成为一个和谐的有机体。他首先把它交给《弗雷泽杂志》（*Fraser's Magazine*）的编辑，但编辑不敢发表，认为这些诗有触犯维多利亚女王的自负之嫌。敏感的诗人决定自己出版。他把它改造成了“波斯花园中的一朵伊壁鸠鲁式的田园诗”。

1859年1月15日，由诗人出资、贝尔纳卡里奇（Bernard Quaritch）出版社匿名出版的这部密密麻麻地印在四开本上首尾相接的75首四行诗《柔波集》终于问世。

但它没有引起任何反响，甚至没有刊物注意到它，也没有杂志评论它。它一败涂地；尽管它的定价仅 5 先令，依然无人问津。出版人把它降至 4 便士，甚至减至 1 便士，读者也不为所动。200册书整整齐齐地被搁在廉价书架上。70年后，即1929年，这本当年 1 便士也没人要的小册子，在纽约杰罗姆·克恩（Jerome Kern）拍卖会上，竟升值至8000美元！这真是一个极大的讽刺！

一年之后，这个平装本的小册子，以 1 便士的价格卖出了几本，其余的堆在不起眼的角落里，落满了尘土。又过了很久，拉斐尔前派诗人、画家罗塞蒂（Dante Gabriel Rossetti，1828—1882）在逛旧书摊时无意间发现了这部诗集。他立刻被吸引，并督促所有的朋友和弟子把伦敦所有的旧书店搜寻个遍，网罗这个稀世之宝。一时间，圈内人兴奋至极，开谈无不议论此书。有的认为这部神秘的匿名作品并非译作；有的认为，这是一个不同寻常的骗局。争议使得此书更加扑朔迷离，充满诱人的色彩。史文朋（Algernon Charles Swinburne，1837—1909）和理查德·伯顿（Sir Richard Burtan，1821—1890）也加入其中，使得这种兴头蔓延至文学界的各个角落。

出版界也随之兴奋起来。

1868年，菲茨杰拉德出版了《柔波集》的第 2 版；他把第 1 版的75首诗增至110首，并做了大量的修改，使得内容更加精练，尽管失去了第 1 版的大胆、泼辣，但文笔更加传神了。

1872年，他在第 2 版的基础上，进一步加工修改，删至101首，出版了第 3 版，依然被市场所接受。

1879年，他在第 3 版的基础上做了更大的修改，出版了第4版。此版最为精致，也最为流行。

菲茨杰拉德的这些充满灵性的译文，使得古老的《柔波集》俨然成为当代之作。

尽管此时《柔波集》已深入人心，赢得大众的普遍喜爱，但译者依然保持缄默，拒绝公开承认他是这部作品的译者。甚至在第4版面世时，他依然要求出版商："在该书的任何广告或告示中，一律不得出现我的名字。”

直到他死后的第 6 年，即1889年，出版了第 5 版。此版只是改正了第 4 版中的一个拼写错误，删去了 3 个逗号，把一个字母改成大写，改正了一个明显的印刷错误。之后，重印时，封面上开始出现译者菲茨杰拉德的名字，而他已长眠于地下，无法阻止了。

爱德华·菲茨杰拉德创译《柔波集》历经30年，五番增删。一个半世纪以来，它一直受到文坛的追捧、读者的喜爱，风靡全球，成了世界文学的不朽经典之一。

菲茨杰拉德的成功创译，织造了一件东西方文化浑然融贯的至臻绝品，成为西方文学的经典之作。

爱德华·菲茨杰拉德（Edward Fitzgerald，1809—1883）的辛勤劳动，让《柔波集》绽放出万古不灭的光辉，成为诗人译诗的典范！

这本小诗集在西方世界引起巨大的震动，由此，英文及其他文本的奥马尔·哈亚姆的《柔波集》译文不断涌现。至19世纪末出现了一个百衲本，汇集的英文、法文、德文、意大利文的译本达30余种之多。至今，在书店里，各种版式的《柔波集》应有尽有，既有 5 美分一册的平装本，也有装帧精美的本子。其中一种手绘牛皮封面用皮革装帧并镶嵌珠宝的豪华精装本，价值高达5000美元。可惜，在1912年海难中，它随“泰坦尼克号”一起沉没海底。

《柔波集》已被译成各种不同的文本，人口

仅20万人的冰岛，亦有从菲茨杰拉德转译的《柔波集》。至今，新的译本仍在不断地涌现。在如此众多的译本中，唯有菲茨杰拉德的译文最为成功。他的译文在当时感染了英国世纪末的诗歌情绪，其中的异国情调和悲观主义深刻地影响了19世纪的唯美主义思潮。这些诗至今依然广泛流传，很多篇章被反复引用，甚至变成日常用语。毫不夸张地说，这本小诗集在英国家喻户晓，得到广泛引用。

比如为讽刺食品价格昂贵，一位读者把《柔波集》中的第12首“修订”成下列两行：

一大杯小酒，再加上一个面包
已把你一周的预算耗尽

又如一位女打字员总是出错，她自嘲地在打字机旁贴上《柔波集》的第71首：

指动字成，字成指动；
无论你如何至诚机敏，
也无法反悔抹去半行，
任你洒尽泪水也难洗净。

新一代的迷恋者把《柔波集》推向至高无上的经典名著行列。

可以说，它不仅是一部诗集、一句口号，一种针对一切伪装和僵化而佩带着韵律的反抗，对于摆脱常规的人，这里已经成为一个理想的离经叛道之所，由此流溢而出的美酒琼浆，既是对自由精神的滋补，又是自由的鸦片。

菲茨杰拉德最初的手稿已不知去向，残存的几页现在美国，被收藏家罗森巴赫（A.S.W.Rosenbach）珍藏。但它的后裔却数不胜数，仅《柔波集文献资料汇编》罗列的版本就达300余种之多。哈亚姆这些被长期忽视的冥想及沉思，这些超然物外的情绪，经过菲茨杰拉德不朽的提炼，已经变成轻快的现代警句。这些灵动的词语、轻盈的句子，犹如散落的珍珠变成迷人的项链，佩戴在思想女神的美丽脖颈上。

魅力何来?

它既来自于诗中所彰显的思想观念，也来自于诗中流溢的韵律的精确。有时抑扬顿挫的节奏似乎起主导作用，可是，在你感到困惑时，寓意又用它的明晰和确凿使我们感到安慰。因此，我们无法把二者区分开来，乐感和寓言的完美结合使它们的魅力在这个酸涩的世界里不断地散发出甜蜜的气息。

在这里，思想不再穿着神秘色彩的外衣，人最隐晦最沉重的难题得到轻松的解答；它没有对哀伤的迷恋，也不暗含什么启示。在这里，智慧成为伸手可及的抚慰，而非故作深沉的姿态。它似乎并没有说出什么本质意义上的新东西，但它所传达的气息却是这么热烈，兴奋与平静的比例如此适度，以至于所思所想读起来像是深刻的发现。可以攻击这些都是陈词滥调，但这些充溢着机智、带着独特个性色彩的声音，却牢牢地留驻在你的脑海中，即便最不敏感的耳朵也能感受到它的抑扬顿挫。

就这样，一个远古波斯人通过相隔700年之久、相距万里之遥的19世纪陌生英国绅士的声音，输入永恒不变的感官情绪。而它散发出的深邃与旋律却没有时日和尺距，它既及时又无限，天涯咫尺。新一代的读者一经发现，总会给它注入新的生机。它如一块跳板，让读者逃离困惑，跃入希望的殿堂，使得精神紧贴心灵的需求，并从消极的怀疑步入积极的进取。

《柔波集》已成为世界上必读50本书籍中信仰类的首本，批注为：“信仰的归宿，灵魂的良药！”

第1版

柔波集

集校版全集

Rubaiyat of Omar Khayyarm

1859年第1版

[波斯] 奥马尔·哈亚姆 著
[英] 爱德华·菲茨杰拉德 英译
文爱艺 译

序

文爱艺

《柔波集》（*Rubáiyát*）原本是古波斯最古老的诗歌体裁样式，历史上用该体裁写作的作者众多，最出名的当属奥马尔·哈亚姆创作的“柔波”。作为一种体裁，“柔波”已经与这位作者紧密联系在一起了。

《柔波集》有“世界文学瑰宝”之称，是世界上被翻译得最多的诗集。

奥马尔·哈亚姆（波斯文：عمر خیام，拉丁文：Omar Khayyám，英文：Omar Khayyam，全名：Ghiyáth al-Din Abul Fateh Omar Ibn Ibráhim al-khayyám，又有莪默·伽亚谟、奥马开俨、欧玛尔·海亚姆、奥玛珈音等译名，1048年5月18日—1122年12月4日），生在11世纪的波斯，相当于中国的北宋时期。哈亚姆少年时期师从大学者伊玛姆·穆瓦法克（lmán Mowaffak），受到良好的早期教育；中年时期，任职于宫廷，获得上司的器重。他对天文学、数学研究精深，24岁被任命为“天官”，参与修订日历。他一生写过很有价值的学术论文，精通历史、法学和医学。

哈亚姆的创作生前并不出名，在他去世后的几百年内，他的这些诗已被淡忘。英国人菲茨杰拉德（Edward FitzGerald）对他的《柔波集》发生了兴趣，以极其自由的方式“译出”了英国式“柔波”（Rubái）并编成集。这引起了人们对原作的注意，译作也成为英国诗歌中的精品并获得世界性声誉，在很多国家，成了不断迻译的对象。

菲茨杰拉德译文的成功在世界范围内掀起了迻译《柔波集》高潮。据伊朗学者的粗略统计，《柔波集》有66种英文译本，19种法文译本，16种德文译本，12种乌尔都文译本，9种阿拉伯文译本，7种意大利文译本，6种土耳其文，4种俄文译本，3种译本丹麦文译本，3种瑞典文译本，2种亚美尼亚文译本，2种冰岛文译本，1种拉丁文译本。译本之多可谓举世无双，版本、印数已难统计，仅纽约图书馆便藏有500

多种版本，至今仍有新的译本不断涌现。这在诗歌史、翻译史、文学史上都是独一无二的。

这本价值与它的厚度成反比的伟大著作不仅滋养了历代文人学者，也引起诸多画家的注意，为其插画的绘画大师无数，随手翻阅，著名的就有：William Morris（1834—1896）、Ronald Edmund Balfour(1896—1941)、Edmund Joseph Sullivan(1869—1933)、EdmundDulac(1882—1953)、Arthur Szyk(1897—1951)、John YungeBateman(1897—1971)、George Buday(1907—1990)、StephenFrederick Gooden(1892—1955)、William Andrew Pogany(1882—1955)、Charles de Sousy Ricketts(1866—1931)、Charles Robinson(1870—1937)、Robert Stewart Sherriffs(1906—1960)、Charles William Stewart(1915—2001)……灿若星河……

本书收入萨基斯·喀特查都里安为1859第一版全集创作的的7幅彩画插图。

萨基斯·喀特查都里安（Sarkis Katchadourian，1896－1947）的插画特别为此版定制，现由旧金山乔治·马蒂基安收藏，用五色重印；最初刻板由Meehan-Tooker公司制作，H.Wolff Book Manufacturing公司联合出版，A.P.TEDESCO公司排版设计完成。

萨基斯·喀特查都里安是波斯现代伟大的艺术家之一，他出生在伊朗，在罗马、巴黎和慕尼黑接受教育。就像他的人生，他的艺术也是世界性的。他第一次赢得世界的关注是他在伊斯法罕宫殿绘制的充满浪漫气息的壁画。这幅壁画是他多年的成果，给他带来艺术界和考古界的声望。他一生都在世界各国游走和绘画，他的画作也被各地的喜爱者收藏。

他的艺术之路始于罗马的里奇美术学院（Reggio Institute de Belle Arti），接下来是巴黎装饰艺术学院（Ecole des Arts Decoratifs），之后又转道慕尼黑。

他倾注一生大量的心血来诠释波斯艺术的精髓，由他来表现波斯艺术的伟大杰作之一《柔波集》是最合适的，这是一部名符其实的配有精妙绘图的世界名著。他对波斯文化的理解和欣赏使他的这版《柔波集》的画作特别精准和真实。

菲茨杰拉德对奥马尔·哈亚姆（Omar Khayyam）四行诗那令人惊叹的精美绝伦的诠释，在喀特查都里安栩栩如生富有韵律的插画里，与这部情感丰沛的诗卷，配合得天衣无缝。

从欧洲成功起步之后，艺术家萨基斯·喀特查都里安回到伊朗，又到了印度。在那里，他辛勤工作十年，重现了几乎失传的南亚次大陆早期伟大的壁画艺术。

在印度的工作使他的艺术进一步声名远扬。他的欧洲回归之旅——巴黎、伦敦——使他在艺术和考古上赢得了巨大成功，此后的美国之旅同样引人瞩目。

战时，他停留印度追求壁画艺术的重塑，然而这次旅行却因战争不得不提前结束。1941年他来到纽约，继续他非凡的创造生涯。

全球很多著名的博物馆都收藏了他的作品，比如巴黎的吉美博物馆（Musée Guimet）、特罗卡迪宫殿（Palais de Trocadero）、巴黎帕姆斯娱乐博物馆（Musée Jeux des Paumes）、柏林的国家博物馆（National Museum in Berlin）、斯德哥尔摩的国家博物馆（National Museum in Stockholm）、维也纳的市政博物馆（Vienna's municipal museum）、波士顿艺术博物馆（Boston Museum of Fine Arts）、芝加哥艺术学院（Art Institute of Chicago）、华盛顿国家艺术和自由收藏美术馆（National Collection of Fine Arts and the Freer Galleries）,以及纽约都市艺术博物馆（Metropolitan Museum of Art）。

rubaiyat

I

Awake! for Morning in the Bowl of Night
Has flung the Stone that puts the Stars to Flight:
And Lo! the Hunter of the East has caught
The Sultan's Turret in a Noose of Light.

清醒吧！晨报的石头
已星星般地投进黑暗的碗中[①]：
看吧！阳光之箭把璀璨的光辉
射向苏丹[②]的高瓴。

译注

①阿拉伯的骆驼商队凌晨上路时，以石子投入碗为出发的信号。

②苏丹，Sultán，统治者的称号。

II

Dreaming when Dawn's[①] Left Hand was in the Sky
I heard a Voice within the Tavern[②] cry,
"Awake, my Little ones, and fill the Cup
Before Life's Liquor in its Cup be dry."

黎明的左手刚至空中
我听到一个声音在梦的酒馆里叫喊，
“醒醒吧，我的小家伙，快把杯子斟满
趁生命之酒还没有枯干。”

译注

①when Dawn's，天文学称之为zodiacal light（黄道光亮），赤道

地区日出日落后一至三小时内因地平线下太阳光经空气中的尘埃团的折射而形成的光；经常与银河同时出现在天上。Left，左边的，左侧的；左派的, 左翼；左派，激进分子；含有间接之意。

②Tavern解释为inn，小旅馆。

III

And, as the Cock crew, those who stood before
The Tavern shouted — "Open then the Door.
You know how little while we have to stay,
And, once departed, may return no more."

此时[①]，公鸡已在啼鸣，在旅馆外面
急切等宿的人们喊道：
“快把门打开，我们只有短暂的休眠，
一旦离去，也许再也不能回还。”

译注

①这句表示承接上首诗。

IV

Now the New Year reviving old Desires,
The thoughtful Soul to Solitude retires,
Where the White Hand of Moses on the Bough
Puts out, and Jesus from the Ground suspires.

新春[①]复活了旧时的希望，
沉思的灵魂在孤寂中隐藏，

摩西的素手[②]嫁接上它的枝条，

耶稣从此地发出叹息[③]。

译注

①古波斯以春分日（3月21日）为元旦，即新春之日。

②典出《圣经·出埃及记》第4章第6节："耶和华又对他说：'把手放在怀里'。他把手放在怀里，及至抽出来，不料，手长了大麻疯，有雪那样白。"此花似波斯的藏红花。摩西（Moses）：可兰经说摩西手白如雪，故借喻白花。另外，《旧约·出埃及记》第4章的前五节中提到了"摩西的杖（moses's hand），典出《旧约·出埃及记》第4章1－5节。耶和华对摩西说：'你手里是什么？'他说：'是杖。'耶和华说：'丢在地上。'他一丢下去，就变作蛇，摩西便跑开。典喻神迹。"

③古波斯人认为，耶稣起死回生的法力存在于他的呼吸之中。

V

Iram indeed is gone with all its Rose,
And Jamshyd's Sev'n-ring'd Cup where no one Knows;
But still the Vine her ancient Ruby yields,
And still a Garden by the Water blows.

依兰园[①]的玫瑰消亡无影，
杰木西的七环杯[②]也不知何往；
但葡萄藤里依然流丹绽放，
水畔的鲜花仍旧缤纷遍地。

译注

①依兰园，原文是Iram，古波斯名园，为夏达德王所建，现已湮没在阿拉伯沙漠之中。

②杰木西（Jamshyd），传说中的古波斯王，原意是日之天子，俾什达迪（Pishdadian）王朝的第五世；七环杯为灵杯，象征七天、七海、七行星，为凯克斯鲁（Kaikhosrú）所造，传言得此杯可知去、来、今三世。杯中常盛不死药。

VI

And David's Lips are lock't; but in divine
High piping Pehlevi, with "Wine! Wine! Wine!
Red Wine!" —the Nightingale cries to the Rose
That yellow Cheek of hers to'incarnadine.

大卫[①]的歌唇紧锁；但是夜莺
用神妙的佩雷微语[②]高歌，
“来！来！来！葡萄美酒啊！”
歌声使玫瑰苍白的脸色红艳。

译注

①大卫（David），古代善歌者，传说为古希伯王，典出《圣经·旧约》。

②佩雷微语（Péhlevi），3世纪至7世纪期间通行于波斯的语言，属印欧语系之伊朗语族，介于古波斯语与现代波斯语之间。

VII

Come, fill the Cup, and in the Fire of Spring
The Winter Garment of Repentance fling:
The Bird of Time has but a little way
To fly—and Lo! the Bird is on the Wing.

来吧，把酒杯斟满，在春天的火中
脱去忏悔的冬衣[①]：
时间之鸟[②]无法永久起飞，
现在它已振翅翱翔。

译注

①中国的春分日，公历（Gregorian Calendar）的3月21日是古波斯传统新年（Nawrūz），新年之前的第一个星期三当晚至第二天天亮，波斯人在街上多次点燃火盆，跳过火盆即可驱走疾病和厄运；此风俗源于公元前6世纪的拜火教（Zoroastrianism）。拜火教由古波斯传入中国后发展为祆教和明教。

②时间之鸟，指春天之鸟，喻时光如飞。

VIII

And look — a thousand Blossoms with the Day
Woke — and a thousand scatter'd into Clay:
And this first Summer Month that brings the Rose
Shall take Jamshyd and Kaikobád away.

看哪：千万朵花儿随日绽开
千万朵花儿飘零化尘埃
这带来芬芳玫瑰的夏日，
也使杰木西、凯可巴[①]一去不再来。

译注

①凯可巴（Kaikobád），古波斯第二王统（Kaianians）王朝之第一君主。据菲尔多西《列王纪》，凯可巴死后传位长子凯卡乌斯。凯卡乌斯子西亚沃什避难突朗部，入赘驸马，与突朗公主法兰吉斯生一子，即凯霍斯鲁。凯霍斯鲁后回国承继祖父凯卡乌斯

之王位。凯为巴列维语尊称，意为首领或统治者，凯扬则是凯之复数。后凯扬演变为世间王者之代称。波斯史中凯扬灵光即指世间人君所享有之神恩与福佑，与中国所谓真命天子意同。

IX

But come with old Khayyám, and leave the Lot
Of Kaikobád and Kaikhosrú forgot:
Let Rustum lay about him as he will,
Or Hátim Tai cry Supper—heed them not.

来吧，随老哈亚姆吧，凯可巴大帝、
凯克斯鲁①与我们有什么关系？
让查尔②、鲁士③恣意咆哮去吧，
哈蒂姆④招邀欢筵——也不会叫上你。

译注

①凯克斯鲁（Kaihosrú），凯可巴之孙，即波斯帝国的创建者居鲁士（前？－前529），他于前538年占领巴比伦，释放被俘者，灭新巴比伦王国。

②查尔（Zál），古波斯英雄。原义是白化病；《列王纪》（Shāhnāma，希伯来语：Sefer Melachim，是《旧约圣经》的一部分，原文用希伯来语书写）记载，这个白化病婴儿被遗弃山中，被大鹏神鸟（simurgh，大地、海洋和天空的结合体，住在知识之树的树顶，曾亲眼目睹世界的三次大毁灭）发现并养大。

③鲁士（Rustam），查尔之子，英勇非凡。

④哈蒂姆（Hátim Tai），公元6世纪阿拉伯塔伊族（Taiy tribe）人。东方贵族，以慷慨著称。

X

With me along some Strip of Herbage strown
That just divides the desert from the sown,
Where name of Slave and Sultan scarce is known,
And pity Sultán Máhmúd on his Throne.

请随我踏上这片狭窄之地，
这儿一边是荒原，一边是播种之域，
囚奴与国王之名到此消失，
尽管穆罕默德[1]安坐在黄金宝座上。

译注

①穆罕默德（Máhmúd，979－1030），阿富汗加兹王朝国王，在位期间以极端专制集权，一生长期征战，并多次入侵印度，将国土面积扩大，至今伊朗、阿富汗、巴基斯坦以及印度西北部的广大区域。为10世纪末叶著名的苏丹。

XI

Here with a Loaf of Bread beneath the Bough,
A Flask of Wine, a Book of Verse – and Thou
Beside me singing in the Wilderness –
And Wilderness is Paradise enow.

树下，一块面包
一瓶酒，一部诗集——还有你
在荒野为我歌唱——
荒漠也是天堂。

XII

"How sweet is mortal Sovranty!"—think some:
Others—"How blest the Paradise to come!"
Ah, take the Cash in hand and wave the Rest;
Oh, the brave Music of a distant Drum!

有人认为："人间的王权最甜蜜！"
其他人觉得"未来的天堂更令人向往！"
啊，其它的一切都不及手头的现金；
哦，遥远的鼓音①与我何干！

译注

①遥远的鼓音，古波斯皇宫外置有大鼓。

XIII

Look to the Rose that blows about us — "Lo,
Laughing," she says, "into the World I blow:
At once the silken Tassel of my Purse
Tear, and its Treasure on the Garden throw."

请看盛开的芳香玫瑰，
她说道："我刚含笑绽放尘世，
转瞬我的锦囊便碎裂，
囊中的珍宝只能散落无痕。"

XIV

The Worldly Hope men set their Hearts upon
Turns Ashes—or it prospers; and anon,

Like Snow upon the Desert's dusty Face
Lighting a little Hour or two—is gone.

人所神往的希求
瞬间云烟成灰；或许经历繁华，然而
如同飘雪覆盖的沙漠，
只闪现一两刻的明辉。

XV

And those who husbanded the Golden Grain,
And those who flung it to the Winds like Rain,
Alike to no such aureate Earth are turn'd
As, buried once, Men want dug up again.

节谷如金玉，
挥金如雨泥，
回身如大梦，
墓又被掘启。

XVI

Think, in this batter'd Caravanserai
Whose Doorways are alternate Night and Day,
How Sultán after Sultán with his Pomp
Abode his Hour or two, and went his way.

天地飘摇逆旅，
昼夜门户交替，

多少荣华富贵，
匆匆而后离去。

XVII

They say the Lion and the Lizard keep
The Courts where Jamshyd gloried and drank deep;
And Bahrám, that great Hunter—the Wild Ass
Stamps o'er his Head, and he lies fast asleep.

杰木西豪饮的宫殿[①]
如今是猛狮蜥蜴游弋之地；
巴拉姆国王[②]，
野驴踩过他的头，也惊不醒他的深梦。

译注

①指现在位于法尔斯省省会色拉子东北面的波斯波利斯。该城又称为塔赫特·伊·杰木西，意为“杰木西的御座”。现在依然存在一些遗迹。

②巴拉姆（Bahrám），古波斯萨山（Sassanian）王朝（226—642）第14任君主，软弱，好色，曾造七城，涂七色，以七个美女居之，讲七种故事。他在一次捕猎野驴的时候，不小心连人带马栽进山洞。

XVIII

I sometimes think that never blows so red
The Rose as where some buried Cæsar bled;
That every Hyacinth the Garden wears

Dropt in its Lap from some once lovely Head.

古往今来的玫瑰，

属凯撒[①]葬身处的最红；

曾朵朵招展的玉簪儿[②]，

都根植于美女的尸中。

译注

①凯撒（公元前101－公元前44），古罗马执政官，号称凯撒大帝，被刺身亡。

②直译为风信子，一种花。风信子（Hyacinthus orientalis），出自古希腊神话：太阳神（Apollo）和西风神（Zephyrus）同时向美少年雅辛托斯（Hyacinth）求爱，雅辛托斯选择了太阳神，嫉妒的西风神将自己的爱人带走，死者从血泊中开出花儿并重生。故风信子有爱情、重生、春天之含义。

XIX

And this delightful herb whose tender Green

Fledges the River's Lip on which we lean—

Ah, lean upon it lightly! for who knows

From what once lovely Lip it springs unseen!

河畔青青草，

我们枕之眠，

莫要压伤它，

来自美唇边！

XX

Ah, my Belovéd, fill the Cup that clears
TO-DAY of past Regrets and future Fears—
To-morrow?—Why, To-morrow I may be
Myself with Yesterday's Sev'n Thousand Years.

噢，我亲爱的，请斟满今日之杯
浇除那昨日之悔和来日之愁，
唉，明天！也许，明天
我已归入尘土①。

译注

①原文意为“归入昨日的七千岁”，古波斯人认为地球的年龄为七千年，此处引申意为人死后归于尘土，故译为“我已归入尘土”。法文译者尼古拉认为，七千年是指亚当创造人类至今的时间。

XXI

Lo! some we loved, the loveliest and best
That Time and Fate of all their Vintage prest,
Have drunk their Cup a Round or two before,
And one by one crept silently to Rest.

瞧！我们所钟爱的人间之美，
时间和命运把它从葡萄中榨成酒浆，
我们从中仅饮得三杯两盏，
瞬间即无声无息地永久长眠。

XXII

And we, that now make merry in the Room
They left, and Summer dresses in new Bloom,
Ourselves must we beneath the Couch of Earth
Descend, ourselves to make a Couch — for whom?

秾芳盛满了古人的华堂，
他们走了，我们尽情地在此盛装欢畅，
我们也将入土长眠，
接下来——又是谁在我们的上面狂欢？

XXIII

Ah, make the most of what we yet may spend,
Before we too into the Dust Descend;
Dust into Dust, and under Dust, to lie,
Sans[①] Wine, sans Song, sans Singer, and — sans End!

哎，趁我们入土之前，
尽情地享受人间；
有朝一日，尘归尘，土归土，
歌声美酒，永远也不能同眠！

译注

①Sans，源自法文的古英语，意为：without。

XXIV

Alike for those who for TO-DAY prepare,
And those that after a TO-MORROW stare,

A Muezzin from the Tower of Darkness cries
"Fools! your Reward is neither Here nor There!"

有人终日奔波忙碌，
有人乞求来生成就，
敲钟人[①]从黑暗之塔[②]中呼喊：
“蠢人！报偿无处可求。”

译注

①原文是Muezzín，意为清真寺塔楼上的守钟人，每天在指定的时刻敲钟叫信徒们祈祷。

②黑暗之塔，喻不可知的命运。

XXV

Why, all the Saints and Sages who discuss'd
Of the Two Worlds so learnedly, are thrust
Like foolish Prophets forth; their Words to Scorn
Are scatter'd, and their Mouths are stopt with Dust.

自古高谈阔论的圣贤，
惯会说古论今，
一旦口被尘封，只会自嘲声声，
同江湖预言者没有两样。

XXVI

Oh, come with old Khayyám, and leave the Wise
To talk; one thing is certain, that Life flies;

One thing is certain, and the Rest is Lies;
The Flower that once has blown for ever dies.

哦，老亚姆，智者千言
只有一事无疑——此生如飞，
余者皆是谎言；
花开之后，便是永远的凋亡。

XXVII

Myself when young did eagerly frequent
Doctor and Saint, and heard great Argument
About it and about: but evermore
Came out by the same Door as in I went.

青春时分，我曾热切地
拜访名流圣人，倾听谈生论死的
高论；但我返归时
依然只能原路走回。

XXVIII

With them the Seed of Wisdom did I sow,
And with my own hand labour'd it to grow:
And this was all the Harvest that I reap'd—
"I came like Water, and like Wind I go."

我学会了播种智慧，
并亲手培植它吐穗；

而今收获的却只有

“来如流水，逝如风吹[①]。”

译注

①意为：“我正在风儿的手中消逝。”古波斯诗人法里德·阿尔-丁·阿塔尔（Farid od-Din Attar，约1142—约1220）记载莫尔克被杀时吟叹此句。

XXIX

Into this Universe, and *why* not knowing,
Nor *whence*, like Water willy-nilly flowing:
And out of it, as Wind along the Waste,
I know not *whither*, willy-nilly blowing.

飘然入世，如水不由自主，
不知为何来，亦不知来自何处；
飘然出世，如风不能停留，
吹过沙丘，亦不知飘向哪里。

XXX

What, without asking, hither hurried *whence*?
And, without asking, *whither* hurried hence!
Another and another Cup to drown
The Memory of this Impertinence!

莫问何处来，
莫问哪里去！
狂欢饮禁酒，
淹没此记忆！

XXXI

Up from Earth's Centre through the seventh Gate
I rose, and on the Throne of Saturn sate,
And many Knots unravel'd by the Road;
But not the Knot of Human Death and Fate.

从大地的心中腾空而起，
飞过七重天坐上土星龙椅[①]，
沿途巧解无数难破之谜；
但不是人类死亡和命运的情结。

译注

①波斯神话中，视土星为第七重天的主宰。

XXXII

There was a Door to which I found no Key:
There was a Veil past which I could not see:
Some little Talk awhile of ME and THEE[①];
There seemed—and then no more of THEE, and ME.

门紧锁，我找不到钥匙，
帷幕紧，我看不到内幕；
仔细听，你我被人指点，
不多时，你我都将消失。

译注

①我（ME）指个体的存在，你（THEE）指芸芸众生。

XXXIII

Then to the rolling Heav'n itself I cried,
Asking, "What lamp had Destiny to guide
Her little Children stumbling in the Dark?"
And—"A blind understanding!" Heav'n replied.

然后我向滚动的苍天呼号，
问："什么样的灯引导命运
她那在黑暗中摸索的孩子？"
"盲目的悟性！"天上的回答。

XXXIV

Then to this earthen Bowl did I adjourn
My Lip the secret Well of Life to learn:
And Lip to Lip it murmur'd—"While you live,
Drink!—for once dead you never shall return."

我的唇俯就在钵边，
学习生活之泉的秘密：
两唇相吻，酒唇低语，
"快快畅饮，死后难聚。"

XXXV

I think the Vessel, that with fugitive
Articulation answer'd, once did live,
And merry-make; and the cold Lip I kiss'd

How many Kisses might it take—and give[1]!

幽幽低语的这个酒杯
曾经鲜活痛饮在人间；
哎！我吻过的唇是多么的冰冷，
不知它曾接受过多少回！

译注

①古波斯诗人法里德·阿尔一丁·阿塔尔（Farid od-Din Attar，约1142—约1220）在诗中写道:旅人用双手托起泉水喝，甘甜，当他用路人留下的陶罐来饮，同样的水却饮出了苦味。来自天空的声音告诉他，现在的陶土，曾经也是鲜活的生命，万物流转，当化为尘土，制为容器，仍无法消弭残留于土中的苦涩。

XXXVI

For in the Market-place, one Dusk of Day,
I watch'd the Potter thumping his wet Clay:
And with its all obliterated Tongue
It murmur'd—"Gently, Brother, gently, pray !"

在市集上，一天黄昏，
我看见陶工用力捣他的湿土：
陶土用它从未开启的舌传出微弱的
哀号——“轻点，兄弟，轻点，求你！”

XXXVII

One Moment in Annihilation's Waste,
One Moment, of the Well of Life to taste—

The Stars are setting and the Caravan
Starts for the dawn of Nothing – Oh, make haste!

片刻的停留这瞬间的滋味
细品这荒漠甘泉的生命之水——
幻影商队从无中来回无中去
黎明没有开始——噢，快饮吧！

XXXVIII

Ah, fill the Cup--what boots it to repeat
How Time is slipping underneath our Feet:
Unborn TO-MORROW and dead YESTERDAY,
Why fret about them if TO-DAY be sweet!

啊，斟满酒杯；反复唠叨
时间如何在我们的脚下流逝又有何益：
昨日已去，明朝未至，
为何为他们发愁，如果今天甜蜜！

XXXIX

How long, how long, in infinite Pursuit
Of This and That endeavour and dispute?
Better be merry with the fruitful Grape
Than sadden after none, or bitter, Fruit.

多久，多久，在无限追求
这样那样的努力和争议？

一杯美酒在手，

何必空自担忧。

XL

You know, my Friends, how long since in my House

For a new Marriage I did make Carouse:

Divorced old barren Reason from my Bed,

And took the Daughter of the Vine to Spouse.

你知道，我的朋友，

我在家中举行盛宴；

我休了不孕的理性，

迎来葡萄的女儿[①]做我的新娘。

译注

①葡萄的女儿，喻指葡萄酒。

XLI

For "IS" and "IS-NOT" though *with* Rule and Line,

And "UP-AND-DOWN" *without*, I could define,

I yet in all I only cared to know,

Was never deep in anything but – Wine.

虽然可以按几何原理判断正误，

虽然可以按逻辑区分兴衰荣辱，

但在人欲探究的一切中，

除酒之外我一无所获。

XLII

And lately, by the Tavern Door agape,
Came stealing through the Dusk an Angel Shape,
Bearing a vessel on his Shoulder; and
He bid me taste of it; and 'twas—the Grape!

不久前，在酒店门口，
暮色中悄悄走来一位天使，
肩上扛着土瓶，他让我品尝
瓶中之物——原来是葡萄美酒！

XLIII

The Grape that can with Logic absolute
The Two-and-Seventy jarring Sects confute:
The subtle Alchemist that in a Trice
Life's leaden Metal into Gold transmute.

葡萄美酒，你以绝对的辩才
令纷争的教派哑口无言；
这狡猾的的炼金师，
瞬间把生活之铅点化成金。

XLIV

The mighty Mahmúd, the victorious Lord,
That all the misbelieving and black Horde
Of Fears and Sorrows that infest the Soul

Scatters and slays with his enchanted Sword.

你是崇高的胜利之主穆罕默德，
你驱除一切妖魔鬼怪，
那入侵鬼魂的悲伤恐惧
在你的利剑下都纷纷逃窜。

XLV

But leave the Wise to wrangle, and with me
The Quarrel of the Universe let be:
And, in some corner of the hubbub coucht,
Make Game of that which makes as much of Thee.

远离这些聪明的穷斗争吵，
令宇宙间的不和与我同行：
在喧哗中的某个角落蹲下，
把取笑你的人尽情地嘲弄。

XLVI

For in and out, above, about, below,
'Tis nothing but a Magic Shadow-show,
Play'd in a Box whose Candle is the Sun,
Round which we Phantom Figures come and go.

进进出出，上上下下，
只不过是魔术阴影显现，
那蜡烛里闪出的日光

回合的我们幻影来来去去。

XLVII

And if the Wine you drink, the Lip you press,
End in the Nothing all Things end in — Yes —
Then fancy while Thou art, Thou art but what
Thou shalt be — Nothing — thou shalt not be less.

如果说美酒和美唇，
都将归入梦境；
想想，此刻之你与未来之你
又有何种区别。

XLVIII

While the Rose blows along the River Brink,
With old Khayyám the Ruby Vintage drink:
And when the Angel with his darker Draught
Draws up to Thee — take that, and do not shrink.

堤岸的玫瑰盛开，
映衬着老哈亚姆殷红的美酒：
天使浓情敬你
你接着，有什么值得退缩犹豫。

XLVIX

Tis all a Chequer-board of Nights and Days

Where Destiny with Men for Pieces plays:
Hither and thither moves, and mates, and slays,
And one by one back in the Closet lays.

日夜不过是黑白相间的棋盘
天意把我们当着可怜的棋子玩：
任它如何纵横拼杀，
最终都将归于匣中长眠。

L

The Ball no Question makes of Ayes and Noes,
But Right or Left, as strikes the Player goes;
And He that toss'd Thee down into the Field,
He knows about it all—HE knows—HE knows!

球只能唯命是从，
一任击打者随意抛弄；
把你抛落地上，
他还要说他自有他的道理！

LI

The Moving Finger writes; and, having writ,
Moves on: nor all thy Piety nor Wit
Shall lure it back to cancel half a Line,
Nor all thy Tears wash out a Word of it.

指动字成，字成指动；

无论你如何至诚机敏，
也无法反悔抹去半行，
任你洒尽泪水也难洗净。

LII

And that inverted Bowl we call the Sky,
Whereunder crawling coop't we live and die,
Lift not thy hands to *It* for help—for It
Rolls impotently on as Thou or I.

天空是个覆盆，
我们生死其中，
不要俯首向它乞求
它的能力与你我相同。

LIII

With Earth's first Clay They did the Last Man's knead,
And then of the Last Harvest sow'd the Seed:
Yea, the first Morning of Creation wrote
What the Last Dawn of Reckoning shall read.

第一把土塑出的将是最终的人，
最后的收成便是那最初的种子；
开天辟地的文章
写就的是天地闭合时的声音。

LIV

I tell Thee this—When, starting from the Goal,

Over the shoulders of the flaming Foal
Of Heav'n Parwin and Mushtara they flung,
In my predestin'd Plot of Dust and Soul

我告诉你——自诞生起，
他们就把帕尔温①和牟希塔利②
抛过天驹③喷火的肩头，
投入我命定的尘与魂中④⑤。

译注

①帕尔温（Parwin），即昴宿（Pleiades）、金牛（Taurus）星座中的一群小星。

②牟希塔利（Mushtarí），即木星（Jupiter）。

③天驹，喻太阳。

④此首诗的内容涉及星象学，是占星术的诗艺表达，太阳所在之处，定人吉凶，此乃迷信之语。

⑤原版第4行，在第1、2、4、5版中皆无标点，唯独第3版有一个句号。按意译此诗与下一首可连读。

LV

The Vine had struck a Fibre; which about
If clings my Being—let the Stiff flout;
Of my Base Metal may be filed a Key,
That shall unlock the Door he howls without.

葡萄生了根，将要与我结缘——
让托钵僧①嘲笑吧；
从我这贱躯中铸一把钥匙，
可把他咆哮不至的门打开。

译注

①托钵僧（Dervish），苏菲派穆斯林苦行者，自身又有很多分支，核心特征是：培养谦卑之心，乞讨为生。乞之所得分若干份，与其他人分享。他们对奥马尔·哈亚姆又恨又怕，因为他嘲弄了他们的信仰。

LVI

And this I know: whether the one True Light,
Kindle to Love, or Wrath consume me quite,
One Glimpse of it within the Tavern caught
Better than in the Temple lost outright.

我知道：无论是欲火燃烧，
还是天怒之火焚我身，
如能在这酒店里看一眼，
胜似在神殿里求睹一生。

LVII

Oh Thou who didst with Pitfall and with Gin
Beset the Road I was to wander in,
Thou wilt not with Predestination round
Enmesh me, and impute my Fall to Sin?

你呀[1]，在我彷徨的徘徊途中
布满美酒和陷阱，
撒下命定的罪孽罗网，
又把堕落的罪名加在我的身上！

译注

①你，指上帝。

LVIII

Oh Thou, who Man of baser Earth didst make,
And who with Eden didst devise the Snake:
For all the Sin wherewith the Face of Man
Is blacken'd, Man's Forgiveness give—and take!

你呀[①]，你用污泥浊水造人，
设伊甸园又引入毒蛇[②]；
人的面目被你污以罪孽，
你宽恕人，其实你已被人宽恕！

译注

①指上帝。此诗与第80首同为诅咒上帝之作。

②典出《圣经·创世纪》，上帝在伊甸之东建乐园让人类始祖亚当和夏娃居住。但在园中还有一条引夏娃偷吃禁果的蛇。

***

KUZA-NÁMA

酒壶之歌[①]

译注：

①第59首至第66首，第1版中冠以“KUZA-NÁMA”之名，意为“陶器篇”，原书其余各版都与全文用一长条*号线隔开，可视为一组诗；为读者了然，笔者意译为“酒壶之歌”。

LIX

Listen again. One Evening at the Close
Of Ramazán, ere the better Moon arose,
In that old Potter's shop I stood alone
With the clay Population round in Rows.

再听一遍。斋月①将尽的晚上
趁着姣美的月亮还没有出现，
我独自站在老陶工的店，
陶国成员环绕在我的身边②。

译注

①斋月（Ramazan），伊斯兰教历的九月是信徒们的封斋期，皆清斋断食。斋月从九月见新月那天开始，到下次看到新月结束，斋月，波斯语：Ramazān, 英语：Ramadan，阿拉伯语：رمضان
رمضا。

②陶人制器的比喻，为外国人常用，参看《圣经·罗马人书》第九章第二十一节。

LX

And strange to tell, among that Earthen Lot
Some could articulate, while others not:
And suddenly one more impatient cried—
"Who *is* the Potter, pray, and who the Pot?"

而且，说来奇怪，陶土中
一些能够表达，另一些则无言：
突然一个不耐烦的叫道——
“谁是陶工，谁是陶器？”

LXI

Then said another—"Surely not in vain
My Substance from the common Earth was ta'en,
That He who subtly wrought me into Shape
Should stamp me back to common Earth again."

然后另一个说：“当然没有白费
我从共同的地球物质中来
他把我巧妙地锻造成形
应该杜绝我再次回归原位。”

LXII

Another said—"Why, ne'er a peevish Boy,
Would break the Bowl from which he drank in Joy;
Shall He that *made* the Vessel in pure Love
And Fansy, in an after Rage destroy!

另一个说：“为什么，游手好闲的玩童，
也不会打破他喝的开怀杯，
为爱而作的器皿
怎能在愤怒中摧毁！”

LXIII

None answer'd this; but after Silence spake
A Vessel of a more ungainly Make:
"They sneer at me for leaning all awry;

What? did the Hand then of the Potter shake? "

没有谁回答，沉默片刻，
外形古怪的开口：
“世人嘲笑我丑陋——
嗯？难道是因为陶工的手曾颤抖？”

LXIV

Said one—"Folks of a surly Tapster tell,
And daub his Visage with the Smoke of Hell;
They talk of some strict Testing of us—Pish!
He's a Good Fellow, and 'twill all be well."

又一个道：“伙计们说起阴沉的塔普斯特①，
用地狱的烟雾涂抹他的面貌；
他们说我们经得起严格的测试，呸！
他是个好人，这决不会错。”

译注

①塔普斯特（Tapster），酒保。

LXV

Then said another with a long-drawn Sigh,
"My Clay with long oblivion is gone dry:
But, fill me with the old familiar Juice,
Methinks I might recover by-and-bye!"

然后另一个长长的叹息道，
“我在长久的忘却中已经干裂；
我只求亲热的酒浆装满我身，
我想我很快就会复活。”

LXVI

So, while the Vessels one by one were speaking,
One spied the little Crescent all were seeking:
And then they jogg'd each other, "Brother! Brother!
Hark to the Porter's Shoulder-knot a-creaking!"

陶瓶们纷纷倾谈，
翘望的新月[①]已出斋露面；
他们互相转告：“朋友！朋友！
搬酒人的垫肩已吱吱作响[②]！”

译注

①Little moon, 意为新月Little cresent moon；伊斯兰教历（阴历）九月封斋，第29天后，如见新月，第二天即开斋，否则便推迟一天。

②陶罐经过搬运人的搬运，进入人世，又能接触到酒浆。

***

LXVII

Ah, with the Grape my fading Life provide,
And wash my Body whence the Life has died,
And in a Windingsheet of Vineleaf wrapt,
So bury me by some sweet Gardenside.

哎，我生将谢，请为我准备酒浆，
在我死后，请洗涤我的皮囊，
让落叶轻轻地把我覆盖，
把我埋在甜蜜的花园。

LXVIII

That ev'n my buried Ashes such a Snare
Of Perfume shall fling up into the Air,
As not a True Believer passing by
But shall be overtaken unaware.

我的遗体虽然已被埋葬，
但它依然在土中哺育葡萄，
那硕果累累的卷须
无意间把虔诚之徒缠绕。

LXIX

Indeed, the Idols I have loved so long
Have done my Credit in Men's Eye much wrong:
Have drown'd my Honour in a shallow Cup,
And sold my Reputation for a Song.

我热爱的这些偶像
令我在世上的眼中蒙羞；
把虚名换成歌声吧，
让光荣消融在杯中。

LXX

Indeed, indeed, Repentance oft before
I swore—but was I sober when I swore?
And then and then came Spring, and Rose-in-hand
My thread-bare Penitence a-pieces tore.

的确，的确，我曾经常忏悔——
但那时我是否清醒？
春风一度，玫瑰在手，
我的忏悔又随风飘飞。

LXXI

And much as Wine has play'd the Infidel,
And robb'd me of my Robe of Honour—well,
I often wonder what the Vintners buy
One half so precious as the Goods they sell.

尽管酒色背信弃义，
总是剥去我体面的外衣，
但是我常想：有什么
比酒贩卖出的酒更为珍奇？

LXXII

Alas, that Spring should vanish with the Rose!
That Youth's sweet-scented Manuscript should close!
The Nightingale that in the Branches sang,
Ah, whence, and whither flown again, who knows!

唉，春天和玫瑰一同消亡！
芬芳的青春手稿也将合上！
夜莺在花枝间娇啼曼唱，
谁能知道她来自哪里，又飞向何方！

LXXIII

Ah, Love! could thou and I with Fate conspire
To grasp this sorry Scheme of Things entire,
Would not we shatter it to bits—and then
Re-mould it nearer to the Heart's Desire!

爱！你我他若能同心
把握住这尘世的不幸，
我们就无须把它砸碎
再造一个世界。

LXXIV

Ah, Moon of my Delight who know'st no wane,
The Moon of Heav'n is rising once again:
How oft hereafter rising shall she look

Through this same Garden after me — in vain!

我的欢乐之月啊，你的明辉永不会减弱，
看天上的月亮又一次升起：
当你再光临此园时，
恐怕我已再难寻觅！

LXXV

And when Thyself with shining Foot shall pass
Among the Guests Star-scatter'd on The Grass,
And in Thy joyous Errand reach the Spot
Where I made one — turn down an empty Glass!

迈着你闪亮的脚
穿梭在草地上寻欢的群客之中，
欣然地走到我曾坐过的地方，
朋友，请为我祭酒一觞！

TAMÁM SHUD

结束

第2版

柔波集

集校版全集

Rubaiyat of Omar Khayyarm

1868年第2版

[波斯] 奥马尔·哈亚姆 著
[英] 爱德华·菲茨杰拉德 英译
文爱艺 译

THE RUBAIYAT
OF OMAR KHAYYAM

I

Wake! For the Sun behind yon Eastern height
Has chased the Session of the Stars from Night,
And, to the field of Heav'n ascending, strikes
The Sultán's Turret with a Shaft of Light.

醒醒！阳光从遥远东方的高山背后
已把聚会的星从夜间驱逐，
而且，它不断的上升，把光辉
射向苏丹①的高瓴。

译注

①苏丹，Sultán，统治者的称号。

II

Before the phantom of False morning died,
Methought a Voice within the Tavern cried,
When all the Temple is prepared within,
"Why lags the drowsy Worshipper outside?"

晨光①在幻影降临前消逝，
旅馆②里似乎有人呼喊：
“神殿已准备就绪，
参拜人为何在外面拖延？”

译注

①False morning died，即false dawn，天文学称之为zodiacal light（黄道光亮），赤道地区日出日落后一至三小时内因地平线下太阳光经空气中的尘

埃团的折射而形成的光；经常与银河同时出现在天上。

②Tavern解释为inn，小旅馆，与下句Temple对比呼应。

III

And, as the Cock crew, those who stood before
The Tavern shouted—"Open then the Door!
You know how little while we have to stay,
"And, once departed, may return no more."

此时[①]，公鸡已在啼鸣，在旅馆外面
急切等宿的人们喊道：
“快把门打开，我们只有短暂的休眠，
一旦离去，也许再也不能回还。”

译注

①这句表示承接上首诗。

IV

Now the New Year reviving old Desires,
The thoughtful Soul to Solitude retires,
Where the WHITE HAND OF MOSES on the Bough
Puts out, and Jesus from the Ground suspires.

新春[①]复活了旧时的希望，
沉思的灵魂在孤寂中隐藏，
摩西的素手[②]嫁接上它的枝条，
耶稣从此地发出叹息[③]。

译注

①古波斯以春分日（3月21日）为元旦，即新春之日。

②典出《圣经·出埃及记》第4章第6节："耶和华又对他说：'把手放在怀里'。他把手放在怀里，及至抽出来，不料，手长了大麻疯，有雪那样白。"此花似波斯的藏红花。摩西（Moses）：可兰经说摩西手白如雪，故借喻白花。另外，《旧约·出埃及记》第4章的前五节中提到了"摩西的杖（moses's hand），典出《旧约·出埃及记》第4章1—5节。耶和华对摩西说：'你手里是什么？'他说：'是杖。'耶和华说：'丢在地上。'他一丢下去，就变作蛇，摩西便跑开。典喻神迹。"

③古波斯人认为，耶稣起死回生的法力存在于他的呼吸之中。

V

Iram indeed is gone with all his Rose,
And Jamshyd's Sev'n-ring'd Cup where no one knows;
But still a Ruby gushes from the Vine,
And many a Garden by the Water blows.

依兰园①的玫瑰消亡无影，
杰木西亚的七环杯②也不知何往；
但葡萄藤里依然流丹绽放，
水畔的鲜花仍旧缤纷遍地。

译注

①依兰园，原文是（Irám），古波斯名园，为夏达德王所建，现已湮没在阿拉伯沙漠之中。

②杰木西（Jamshyd），传说中的古波斯王，原意是日之天子，（Pishdadian）王朝的第五世；七环杯为灵杯，象征七天、七海、七行星，为（Kaikhosrú）所造，传言得此杯可知去、来、今三世。杯中常盛不死药。古波斯人以七为大，以七为至圣，影响至今。

VI

And David's lips are lockt; but in divine
High-piping Péhlevi, with "Wine! Wine! Wine!
"*Red* Wine!" – the Nightingale cries to the Rose
That sallow cheek of her's to incarnadine.

大卫①的歌唇紧锁；但是夜莺
用神妙的佩雷微语②高歌，
“来！来！来！葡萄美酒啊！”
歌声使玫瑰苍白的脸色红艳。

译注

①大卫（David），古代善歌者，传说为古希伯王，典出自《圣经·旧约》。

②佩雷微语（Péhlevi），3世纪至7世纪期间通行于波斯的语言，属印欧语系之伊朗语族，介于古波斯语与现代波斯语之间。

VII

Come, fill the Cup, and in the fire of Spring
Your Winter garment of Repentance fling:
The Bird of Time has but a little way
To flutter – and the Bird is on the Wing.

来吧，把酒杯斟满，在春天的火中①
脱去忏悔的冬衣：
时间之鸟②无法永久起飞，
现在它已振翅翱翔。

译注

①中国的春分日，公历（Gregorian Calendar）的3月21日是古波斯传统新年

（Nawrūz），新年之前的第一个星期三当晚至第二天天亮，波斯人在街上多次点燃火盆，跳过火盆即可驱走疾病和厄运；此风俗源于公元前 6 世纪的拜火教（Zoroastrianism）。拜火教由古波斯传入中国后发展为祆教和明教。

②时间之鸟，指春天之鸟，喻时光如飞。

VIII

Whether at Naishápúr or Babylon,
Whether the Cup with sweet or bitter run,
The Wine of Life keeps oozing drop by drop,
The Leaves of Life keep falling one by one.

无论在内沙布尔①还是在巴比伦②，
莫问杯中物是苦涩还是香醇，
生活之酒芳香不止，
生命之叶枯荣不息。

译注

①内沙布尔（Naishápúr，Nīshāpūr），地名，诗人诞生地，位于今伊朗东北部的中呼罗珊省（波斯语：خراسان, 英语：Razavi Khorasan Province），历史上曾是首府。原是丝绸之路上的重要的关口，曾是当时世界上十大城市之一。13世纪，被蒙古大军攻占。公元1221年，成吉思汗（Ghinggis Khan）的金刀驸马脱忽察儿（Toquchar）在此城被冷箭射杀，公主请求成吉思汗屠城。为不留一个活口，托雷（Tolui）下令将所有被杀之人斩首，首级堆成高山，约有170万人被杀。

②巴比伦（Babylon），古巴比伦王国及新巴比伦王国的都城，位于幼发拉底河东岸的两河流域中心，现位于伊拉克境内。在伊拉克首都巴格达南部约50公里处。传说中的古代世界七大奇观之一的空中花园，即在此处。

IX

Morning a thousand Roses brings, you say;
Yes, but where leaves the Rose of Yesterday?
And this first Summer month that brings the Rose
Shall take Jamshyd and Kaikobád away.

你说：早上带来一千朵玫瑰
可哪儿又是昨天玫瑰的下落？
这带来芬芳玫瑰的夏日，
也使杰木西、凯可巴[①]一去不回。

译注

①凯可巴（Kaikobád），古波斯第二王统（Kaianians）王朝之第一君主。据菲尔多西《列王纪》，凯可巴死后传位长子凯卡乌斯。凯卡乌斯子西亚沃什避难突朗部，入赘驸马，与突朗公主法兰吉斯生一子，即凯霍斯鲁。凯霍斯鲁后回国承继祖父凯卡乌斯之王位。凯为巴列维语尊称，意为首领或统治者，凯扬则是凯之复数。后凯扬演变为世间王者之代称。波斯史中凯扬灵光即指世间人君所享有之神恩与福佑，与中国所谓真命天子意同。

X

Well, let it take them! What have we to do
With Kaikobád the Great, or Kaikhosrú?
Let Rusturn cry "To Battle!" as he likes,
Or Hátim Tai "To Supper!" —heed not you.

消失，随他们消失吧，凯可巴大帝
凯克斯鲁[①]与我们有什么关系？
让查尔[②]、鲁士[③]恣意咆哮“开战吧！”，

哈蒂姆[4]招邀欢筵——也不会叫上你。

译注

①凯克斯鲁（Kaihosrú），凯可巴之孙，即波斯帝国的创建者居鲁士（前？一前529），他于前538年占领巴比伦，释放被俘者，灭新巴比伦王国。

②查尔（Zál），古波斯英雄。原义是白化病；《列王纪》（Shāhnāma,希伯来语:Sefer Melachim，是《旧约圣经》的一部分，原文用希伯来语书写）记载，这个白化病婴儿被遗弃山中，被大鹏神鸟（simurgh，大地、海洋和天空的结合体，住在知识之树的树顶，曾亲眼目睹世界的三次大毁灭）发现并养大。

③鲁士（Rustam），查尔之子，英勇非凡。

④哈蒂姆（Hátim Tai），公元6世纪阿拉伯塔伊族（Taiy tribe）人。东方贵族，以慷慨著称。

XI

With me along the strip of Herbage strown
That just divides the desert from the sown,
Where name of Slave and Sultán is forgot—
And Peace to Máhmúd on his golden Throne!

请随我踏上这片狭窄之地，
这儿一边是荒原，一边是牧场，
因奴与国王之名到此消失，
尽管穆罕默德[1]安坐在黄金宝座上。

译注

①穆罕默德（Máhmúd，979—1030），阿富汗加兹王朝国王，在位期间以极端专制集权，一生长期征战，并多次入侵印度，将国土面积扩大，至今

伊朗、阿富汗、巴基斯坦以及印度西北部的广大区域。为10世纪末叶著名的苏丹。

XII

Here with a little Bread beneath the Bough,
A Flask of Wine, a Book of Verse—and Thou
Beside me singing in the Wilderness—
Oh, Wilderness were Paradise enow!

树荫下一点面包，
一瓶美酒，一卷诗，
荒漠中，有你在我身旁欢歌—
噢，荒原，也是天堂！

XIII

Some for the Glories of This World; and some
Sigh for the Prophet's Paradise to come;
Ah, take the Cash, and let the Promise go,
Nor heed the music of a distant Drum!

有人希图现世的荣耀；
有人希图天国的安宁；
噢，且惜今朝，承诺几何，
远方的鼓音[①]我何须理会！

译注

①远方的鼓音：古波斯皇宫外置有大鼓，用于召集军队；暗喻死亡之声。

XIV

Were it not Folly, Spider-like to spin
The Thread of present Life away to win
What? for ourselves, who know not if we shall
Breathe out the very Breath we now breathe in!

还不是愚蠢，仿效蜘蛛
编织人生之丝企获
什么？谁不知道，我们将
呼出的气，就是我们现在吸入的！

XV

Look to the blowing Rose about us — "Lo,
Laughing," she says, into the world I blow:
"At once the silken tassel of my Purse
Tear, and its Treasure on the Garden throw."

请看盛开的芳香玫瑰，
她说道："我刚含笑绽放尘世，
转瞬我的锦囊便碎裂，
囊中的珍宝只能散落无痕。"

XVI

For those who husbanded the Golden grain,
And those who flung it to the winds like Rain,
Alike to no such aureate Earth are turn'd

As, buried once, Men want dug up again.

节谷如金玉，
挥金如雨泥，
回身如大梦，
墓又被掘启。

XVII

The Worldly Hope men set their Hearts upon
Turns Ashes—or it prospers; and anon,
Like Snow upon the Desert's dusty Face,
Lighting a little hour or two—was gone.

人所神往的希求
瞬间云烟成灰；或许经历繁华，然而
如同飘雪覆盖的沙漠，
只闪现一两刻的明辉。

XVIII

Think, in this batter'd Caravanserai
Whose Portals are alternate Night and Day,
How Sultán after Sultán with his Pomp
Abode his destined Hour, and went his way.

天地飘摇逆旅，
昼夜门户交替，
多少荣华富贵，
匆匆而后离去。

دختر قیصر

XIX

They say the Lion and the Lizard keep
The Courts where Jamshyd gloried and drank deep:
And Bahrám, that great Hunter – the Wild Ass
Stamps o'er his Head, but cannot break his Sleep.

杰木西豪饮的宫殿[①]
如今是猛狮蜥蜴游弋之地；
巴拉姆国王[②]，
野驴踩过他的头，也掠不醒他的深梦。

译注

①指现在位于法尔斯省省会色拉子东北面的波斯波利斯。该城又称为塔赫特·伊·杰木西，意为“杰木西的御座”。现在依然存在一些遗迹。

②巴拉姆（Bahrám），古波斯萨山（Sassanian）王朝（226—642）第14任君主，软弱，好色，曾造七城，涂七色，以七个美女居之，讲七种故事。他在一次捕猎野驴的时候，不小心连人带马栽进山洞。

XX

The Palace that to Heav'n his pillars threw,
And Kings the forehead on his threshold drew –
I saw the solitary Ringdove there,
And "Coo, coo, coo," she cried; and "Coo, coo, coo."

曾经高插云霄的宫柱，
那叩首门前的多少君王——
而我只看到孤独的鸽子在宫中，
“咕咕，咕咕，咕咕地”哭着。

اجل همپایه این زندگی باد
وزین ناز زندگی شرمندگی باد
چو سال انتظار از ده فزون شد
لوای طاقت از هر سو نگون شد
هجوم شوق بر دل پا بیفشرد
شکیب اندر کمندکوب هوس مرد
چو از آغوش شوق این شعله سر زد
پسر این نغمه بر گوش پدر زد
که بر من کی شد همخواب و همجفت
شکیبم طاق گشت از فرقت جفت

XXI

Ah, my Belovéd, fill the Cup that clears
To-day of past Regrets and future Fears:
To-morrow! Why, To-morrow I may he
Myself with Yesterday's Sev'n Thousand Years.

噢，我亲爱的，请斟满今日之杯
浇除那昨日之悔和来日之愁，
唉，明天！也许，明天
我已归入尘土[①]。

译注

①原文意为“归入昨日的七千岁”，古波斯人认为地球的年龄为七千年，此处引申意为人死后归于尘土，故译为“我已归入尘土”。法文译者尼古拉认为，七千年是指亚当创造人类至今的时间。

XXII

For some we loved, the loveliest and the best
That from his Vintage rolling Time has prest,
Have drunk their Cup a Round or two before,
And one by one crept silently to rest.

我们所钟爱的人间之美
时光把它从葡萄中榨成酒浆，
我们从中仅饮得三杯两盏，
瞬间即无声无息地永久长眠。

XXIII

And we, that now make merry in the Room

They left, and Summer dresses in new Bloom,
Ourselves must we beneath the Couch of Earth
Descend, ourselves to make a Couch—for whom?

秾芳盛满了古人的华堂
他们走了，我们尽情地在此盛装欢畅，
我们也将入土长眠
接下来，又是谁在我们的上面狂欢？

XXIV

I sometimes think that never blows so red
The Rose as where some buried Cæsar bled;
That every Hyacinth the Garden wears
Dropt in her Lap from some once lovely Head.

古往今来的玫瑰
凯撒①葬身处的最红；
曾朵朵招展的玉簪儿②
都根植于美女的尸中。

译注

①凯撒（Cæsar，公元前101—公元前44），古罗马执政官，号称凯撒大帝，被刺身亡。

②直译为风信子，一种花。风信子（Hyacinthus orientalis），出自古希腊神话：太阳神（Apollo）和西风神（Zephyrus）同时向美少年雅辛托斯（Hyacinth）求爱，雅辛托斯选择了太阳神，嫉妒的西风神将自己的爱人带走，死者从血泊中开出花儿并重生。故风信子有爱情、重生、春天之含义。

XXV

And this delightful Herb whose living Green
Fledges the River's Lip on which we lean—
Ah, lean upon it lightly! for who knows
From what once lovely Lip it springs unseen!

河畔愉悦草
我们枕之眠，
莫要压伤它
来自美唇边！

XXVI

Ah, make the most of what we yet may spend,
Before we too into the Dust descend;
Dust into Dust, and under Dust, to lie,
Sans[①] Wine, sans Song, sans Singer, and—sans End!

哎，趁我们入土之前，
尽情地享受人间；
有朝一日，尘归尘，土归土，
歌声美酒，永远也不能同眠！

译注

①Sans，源自法文的古英语，意为：without。

XXVII

Alike for those who for TO-DAY prepare,

And those that after some TO-MORROW stare,
A Muezzin from the Tower of Darkness cries,
"Fools! your Reward is neither Here nor There."

有人终日奔波忙碌，
有人乞求来生成就，
敲钟人①从黑暗之塔②中呼喊：
“蠢人！报偿无处可求。”

译注

①原文是（Muezzin），意为清真寺塔楼上的守钟人，每天在指定的时刻敲钟叫信徒们祈祷。

②黑暗之塔，喻不可知的命运。

XXVIII

Another Voice, when I am sleeping, cries,
"The Flower should open with the Morning skies."
And a retreating Whisper, as I wake—
"The Flower that once has blown for ever dies."

另一种声音，在我睡觉的时候，哭着说，
“花应该随着早晨的天空开放。”
醒来时，我却听到缥缈的低语——
“花开之后，便是永远的凋亡。”①

译注

①此诗本版独有；其中第4句跟第1版的第26首的第4句、第4版第5版第63首的第4句相同。

XXIX

Why, all the Saints and Sages who discuss'd
Of the Two Worlds so learnedly, are thrust
Like foolish Prophets forth; their Words to Scorn :
Are scatter'd, and their Mouths are stopt with Dust.

自古高谈阔论的圣贤，
惯会说古论今
一旦口被尘封，只会自嘲声声：
同江湖预言者没有两样。

XXX

Myself when young did eagerly frequent
Doctor and Saint, and heard great argument
About it and about: but evermore
Came out by the same door as in I went.

青春时分，我曾热切地
拜访名流圣人；倾听谈生论死的
高论，但我返归时
依然只能原路走回。

XXXI

With them the seed of Wisdom did I sow,
And with my own hand wrought to make it grow:
And this was all the Harvest that I reap'd—

"I came like Water, and like Wind I go."

我学会了播种智慧，

并亲手培植它吐穗；

而今收获的却只有：

“来如流水，逝如风吹[①]”。

译注

①意为：“我正在风的手中消逝。”古波斯诗人法里德·阿尔-丁·阿塔尔（Farid od-Din Attar，约1142—约1220）记载莫尔克被杀时吟叹此句。

XXXII

Into this Universe, and Why not knowing,

Nor Whence, like Water willy-nilly flowing:

And out of it, as Wind along the Waste,

I know not Whither, willy-nilly blowing.

飘然入世，如水不由自主

不知何来，亦不知来自何处；

飘然出世，如风不能停留，

吹过沙丘，亦不知飘向哪里。

XXXIII

What, without asking, hither hurried Whence?

And, without asking, whither hurried hence!

Ah, contrite Heav'n endowed us with the Vine

To drug the memory of that insolence!

莫问何处来？

莫问哪里去！

悔悟天赐酒

麻醉此记忆！

XXXIV

Up from Earth's Centre through the Seventh Gate
I rose, and on the Throne of Saturn sate,
And many Knots unravel'd by the Road;
But not the Master-Knot of Human Fate.

从大地的心中腾空而起
飞过七天坐上土星高椅①，
沿途巧解无数难破之谜；
但人生这个谜却总也猜不透。

译注

①hurried，土星，波斯神话中，视土星为第七重天的主宰。西方人古代称为Saturnus（拉丁文），为太阳系八大行星之一。至太阳距离（由近到远）位于第六位，体积则仅次于木星，并与木星、天王星及海王星同属气体（类木）行星。土星具有美丽的环带结构，截止2012年已发现62颗卫星，离地球最远。古代中国称之镇星或填星。

XXXV

There was the Door to which I found no Key:
There was the Veil through which I could not see:
Some little talk awhile of ME and THEE

There was—and then no more of THEE and ME[①].

门紧锁，我找不到钥匙，
帷幕紧，我看不到内幕；
仔细听，你我被人指点
不多时，你我都将消失。

译注

①我（ME）指个体的存在，你（THEE）指芸芸众生。

XXXVI

Earth could not answer; nor the Seas that mourn
In flowing Purple, of their Lord forlorn;
Nor Heav'n, with those eternal Signs reveal'd
And hidden by the sleeve of Night and Morn.

地球不能回答，无主的海洋
翻滚着紫波，也无法回答；
上天挥舞的日夜之袖
那永恒的隐现也无解答。

XXXVII

Then of the THEE IN ME who works behind
The Veil of Universe I cried to find
A Lamp to guide me through the Darkness; and
Something then said—"An Understanding blind."

叩问我的神灵
呼唤为我指引
穿越黑暗之灯
只听“盲目之心。”

XXXVIII

Then to the Lip of this poor earthen Urn
I lean'd, the secret Well of Life to learn:
And Lip to Lip it murmur'd—"While you live,
Drink !—for, once dead, you never shall return."

俯就在酒的唇边
探究生之奥秘：
两唇相吻，酒唇低语
“快快畅饮，死后难聚。”

XXXIX

I think the Vessel, that with fugitive
Articulation answer'd, once did live,
And drink; and that impassive Lip I kiss'd,
How many Kisses might it take—and give!

幽幽低语的这个酒杯[①]
曾经鲜活痛饮在人间；
哎！而今我吻着它冷漠的唇，
不知它曾接受过多少回！

احوال ایشان بپرسید گفتند که غذای ما گیاه است از آن این چنین گشته ایم الکه ذوالقرنین
را مهمان کردند حکیمان گرد آمدند و هر یکی حکمتی میگفتند تا نوبت ذوالقرنین رسید وی را گفتند

译注

①古波斯诗人法里德·阿尔-丁·阿塔尔（Farid od-Din Attar，约1142—约1220）在诗中写道：旅人用双手托起泉水喝，甘甜，当他用路人留下的陶罐来饮，同样的水却饮出了苦味。来自天空的声音告诉他，现在的陶土，曾经也是鲜活的生命，万物流转，化为尘土，制为容器，仍无法消弭残留于土中的苦涩。

XL

For I remember stopping by the way
To watch a Potter thumping his wet Clay:
And with its all-obliterated Tongue
It murmur'd—"Gently, Brother, gently, pray!"

我曾经在路途中
看见陶工用力捣土，
陶土用它从未开启的舌传出微弱的
哀号——“轻点，兄弟，轻点，求你！”

XLI

For has not such a Story from of Old
Down Man's successive generations roll'd
Of such a clod of saturated Earth
Cast by the Maker into Human mould?

我们来自泥土
又归于泥土
代代如此

这难道仅是传言？

XLII

And not a drop that from our Cups we throw
On the parcht herbage but may steal below
To quench the fire of Anguish in some Eye
There hidden — far beneath, and long ago.

我们祭洒在焦枯牧草上的美酒
一点一滴潜入地底深处
渗进逝者难瞑的双目
消除它焦灼无解的痛苦。

XLIII

As then the Tulip for her wonted sup
Of Heavenly Vintage lifts her chalice up,
Do you, twin offspring of the soil, till Heav'n
To Earth invert you like an empty Cup.

郁金香仰起花的渴望
天国佳酿举起她的圣杯，
你土壤的孪子，也该如此举杯，
直到天地将你逆转，如倾倒酒杯。

XLIV

Do you, within your little hour of Grace,

The waving Cypress[①] in your Arms enlace,
Before the Mother back into her arms
Fold, and dissolve you in a last embrace.

你，在享受天伦的短暂时刻，
你的手臂缠绕住挥舞着风姿的翠柏
趁大地之母还未把你收回
尽情消受那最后的怀抱。

译注

①cypress，柏属植物（原产北美、欧、亚），柏树；柏树枝，用作哀悼的标志。

XLV

And if the Cup you drink, tile Lip you press,
End in what All begins and ends in—Yes;
Imagine then you are what heretofore
You were--hereafter you shall not be less.

如果说美酒和美唇，
都将归入梦境；
想一想，迄今的你
过去的你，也是如此。

XLVI

So when at last the Angel of the drink

Of Darkness finds you by the river-brink,
And, proffering his Cup, invites your Soul
Forth to your Lips to quaff it—do.not shrink.

如果最后黑酒天使
在冥河之畔找到了你，
而且，向你的灵魂邀杯
畅饮吧，你的唇无须畏缩。

XLVII

And fear not lest Existence closing your
Account, should lose, or know the type no more;
The Eternal Sáki from that Bowl has pour'd
Millions of Bubbles like us, and will pour.

虽然我们不存在了
但生命之火依然
我们不过是酒中的一滴
永恒的造化[1]将不停的斟酌。

译注

①原文是（Sáki），波斯语，原意为托杯斟酒者，引申义为造化，故此意译。

XLVIII

When You and I behind the Veil are past,
Oh but the long long while the World shall last

Which of our Coming and Departure heeds
As much as Ocean of a pebble-cast.

当你我消失之后，
时间依然如故
你我的来去
犹如小石子投入海中。

XLIX

One Moment in Annihilation's Waste,
One Moment, of the Well of Life to taste--
The Stars are setting, and the Caravan
Draws to the Dawn of Nothing—Oh, make haste!

寂灭的荒漠只能片刻湮留，
这瞬间足以品茗生命之井的滋味——
星移斗转，幻影商队已从无中来
又归无中去——噢，快饮吧！

L

Would you that spangle of Existence spend
About THE SECRET— quick about it, Friend!
A Hair, they say, divides the False and True—
And upon what, prithee, does Life depend?

如果你愿意花宝贵的光阴
去探寻人生——朋友，那就去吧！

گرفته ساغر عشرت فرشته رحمت
ز جرعه بر رخ حور و پری گلاب زده

真理和谬误一线之别，
舍此，生活有何凭依？

LI

A Hair, they say, divides the False and True;
Yes; and a single Alif were the clue,
Could you but find it, to the Treasure-house,
And peradventure to THE MASTER too;

真理和谬误一线之隔；
是的；只一个“阿里夫”[①]便至达——
只要你能领悟——
它便引领你归依真主；

译注

①阿里夫，原文是（Alif），阿拉伯字母中的第一个字母，波斯语中发音为（Alef）；伊斯兰教中的真主安拉（Alllah）也以此为字首。印度教梵文经本《薄伽梵歌》(Bhagavad Gītā；英译：Song of God，汉语意译：神之歌、主黑天之歌；薄伽梵歌的字面意思是“主之歌”或“神之歌”，这里的主或者神就是黑天，薄伽梵相当于上帝，梵相当于圣灵。)：“我是所有文字的A字母，我是离合释中的相违释。我是流逝无尽中的永恒，我是面向一切的创造者。”

LII

Whose secret Presence, through Creation's veins
Running Quicksilver-like eludes your pains:

Taking all shapes from Máh to Máhi; and
They change and perish all—but He remains;

他看似无形，却无处不在
如水银般流动，消除你的痛疼；
赋形于万物，从月至鱼[①]
都在变化中消亡；而他永存；

译注

①古波斯神话，万物始于月，而终于鱼。另一说为：我们生活的世界是几经周折背负于鱼背之上的。故古波斯文az māh māhī（从鱼到月），鱼借指大地，月代指天空，喻指世界“从大地到天空”“从低处到高处”。

LIII

A moment guess'd--then back behind the Fold
Immerst of Darkness round the Drama roll'd
Which, for the Pastime of Eternity,
He does Himself contrive, enact, behold.

瞬即闪现瞬即消散
人生如戏黑暗迷茫
各自登场各自观赏
戏如人生终归散场

LIV

But if in vain, down on the stubborn floor

Of Earth, and up to Heav'n's unopening Door,
You gaze To-day, while You are You—how then
To-morrow, You when shall be You no more?

在这无情的大地上，
那重门紧闭的天堂，
今日的你，还可凝视，
明日的你又将怎样？

LV

Oh, plagued no more with Human or Divine,
To-morrow's tangle to itself resign,
And lose your fingers in the tresses of
The Cypress①-slender Minister of Wine.

哦，别再为天上人间烦闷，
明朝的纷繁让风处理，
酒神的长发软如松丝，
请用你的手为它梳理。

译注

①cypress，柏属植物（原产北美、欧、亚），柏树；柏树枝（用作哀悼的标志）；似柏树树种；此处专指柏木属植物，俗名 cypress of shirāz，树高达35米，圆锥形狭长树冠，树冠下缘宽度一般不到总树高的十分之一，气味芳馥。波斯文学中常用来形容女性身躯的亭亭玉立和雄健挺拔的男性身躯，含有“高贵”“自由”之意，树的叶子被用来形容人的头发。

LVI

Waste not your Hour, nor in the vain pursuit
Of This and That endeavour and dispute;
Better he merry with the fruitful Grape
Than sadden after none, or bitter, Fruit.

别浪费光阴，
莫追求虚空；
一杯美酒在手，
何必空自担忧。

LVII

You know, my Friends, how bravely in my House
For a new Marriage I did make Carouse:
Divorced old barren Reason from my Bed,
And took the Daughter of the Vine to Spouse.

你知道，我的朋友
我在家中举行盛筵；
我休了不孕的理性，
迎来葡萄的女儿[①]做我的新娘。

译注

①葡萄的女儿，喻指葡萄酒。

LVIII

For "IS" and "IS NOT" though with Rule and Line
And "UP-AND-DOWN" by Logic I define,
Of all that one should care to fathom, I
Was never deep in anything but—Wine.

虽然可以按几何原理判断正误
虽然可以按逻辑区分兴衰荣辱，
但在人欲探究的一切中
除酒之外我一无所获。

LIX

Ah, but my Computations, People say,
Have squared the Year to human compass, eh?
If so, by striking from the Calendar
Unborn To-morrow and dead Yesterday.

唉，人们说我的推算高明，
我真的重排了岁月了吗？
我只不过是从历史中
勾销了未生的明天和死去的昨天。

LX

And lately, by the Tavern Door agape,
Came shining through the Dusk an Angel Shape

Bearing a Vessel on his Shoulder; and
He bid me taste of it; and 'twas—the Grape!

不久前，在酒店门口，
暮色中走来一位天使，
肩上扛着土瓶，他让我品尝
瓶中之物——原来是葡萄美酒！

LXI

The Grape that can with Logic absolute
The Two-and-Seventy jarring Sects confute:
The sovereign Alchemist that in a trice
Life's leaden metal into Gold transmute.

葡萄美酒，你以绝对的辩才
令纷争的教派[1]哑口无言；
你是至尊的炼金师
瞬间把生活之铅点化成金。

译注

①伊斯兰教传统说法，伊斯兰之教派分裂为73派，其中72派会下火狱，只有一派进乐园。

LXII

The mighty Mahmúd, Allah-breathing Lord,
That all the misbelieving and black Horde
Of Fears and Sorrows that infest the Soul
Scatters before him with his whirlwind Sword.

你是崇高的至圣穆罕默德，

你驱除一切妖魔鬼怪，
那入侵鬼魂的悲伤恐惧
在你的利剑下都纷纷逃窜。

LXIII

Why, be this Juice the growth of God, who dare
Blaspheme the twisted tendril as a Snare?
A Blessing, we should use it, should we not?
And if a Curse--why, then, Who set it there?

如果是上帝酿造此美酒，
谁敢把缠绕的卷须[①]咒成陷阱？
天赐之福，难道我们不应该享用？
是灾祸——那么谁是祸手？

译注

①卷须，植物学名词；植物用来缠绕或附着其它物体的器官，此处指葡萄卷须。

LXIV

I must abjure the Balm of Life, I must,
Scared by some After-reckoning ta'en on trust,
Or lured with Hope of some Diviner Drink,
When the frail Cup is crumbled into Dust!

如果害怕来世报应[①]，
或者被来世的神妙迷惑，
我一定断掉此杯，
但要等我死了以后！

译注

①来世报应，回教认为今世禁欲，来世得入天堂，有美女和醇酒为伴，反之则下地狱。

LXV

If but the Vine and Love-abjuring Band
Are in the Prophet's Paradise to stand,
Alack, I doubt the Prophet's Paradise
Were empty as the hollow of one's Hand.

如果在先知乐园
只有绝情无欲之徒
唉！我怀疑先知乐园
虚空如同无一长物的手

LXVI

Oh threats of Hell and Hopes of Paradise!
One thing at least is certain—This Life flies:
One thing is certain and the rest is lies;
The Flower that once is blown for ever dies.

哎，无论是天堂还是地狱！
只有一事无疑——此生如飞；
余者皆是谎言；
花开之后，便是永远的凋亡。

LXVII

Strange, is it not? that of the myriads who
Before us pass'd the door of Darkness through,
Not one returns to tell us of the Road,
Which to discover we must travel too.

奇怪，真是奇怪？
不计其数的死者，
却无一人归来，
告知我们该走的路。

LXVIII

The Revelations of Devout and Learn'd
Who rose before us, and as Prophets burn'd,
Are all but Stories, which, awoke from Sleep
They told their fellows, and to Sleep return'd.

先贤圣哲的宣教
不过是痴人说梦，
醒后告别了同伴
匆匆又归梦中。

LXIX

Why, if the Soul can fling the Dust aside,
And naked on the Air of Heaven ride,
Is't not a shame—is't not a shame for him

So long in this Clay suburb to abide?

如果灵魂能抛弃躯体，
赤裸地遨游天地，
那它为什么还要停在其中，
难道它不感到躯体的丑陋？

LXX

But that is but a Tent wherein may rest
A sultan to the realm of Death addrest;
The Sultan rises, and the dark Ferrásh
Strikes, and prepares it for another guest.

这个只供小憩一时的天幕，
在苏丹奔赴冥国时开启；
黑暗的命运①很快关闭，
静待下一位起息。

译注

①原文是（Ferrásh），本意为开启天幕者，此处引申意为造化、命运。

LXXI

I sent my Soul through the Invisible,
Some letter of that After-life to spell:
And after many days my Soul return'd
And said, "Behold, Myself am Heav'n and Hell :"

我把我的灵魂送入幽冥之境，

去翻阅我死后的片言只语；
多天之后我的灵魂归来告知：
“看哪，我自己便是天堂和地狱！”

LXXII

Heav'n but the Vision of fulfill'd Desire,
And Hell the Shadow of a Soul on fire,
Cast on the Darkness into which Ourselves,
So late emerg'd from, shall so soon expire.

天堂是奢望的幻影，
地狱是欲望的虚像，
我们从欲望中现身，
不久将从此处忘形。

LXXIII

We are no other than a moving row
Of visionary Shapes that come and go
Round with this Sun-illumin'd Lantern held
In Midnight by the Master of the Show;

我们不过是一群幻影
绕着灯来去匆匆
在深更夜半
点燃，在魔术师的手中

LXXIV

Impotent Pieces of the Game He plays
Upon this Chequer-board of Nights and Days;
Hither and thither moves, and checks, and slays;
And one by one back in the Closet lays.

不过是一群可怜的棋子
在昼与夜的棋盘上布局；
任它如何纵横拼杀，
最终都将归于匣中长眠。

LXXV

The Ball no question makes of Ayes and Noes,
But Right or Left as strikes the Player goes;
And He that toss'd you down into the Field,
He knows about it all--HE knows—HE knows!

球只能唯命是从，
一任击打者随意抛弄；
把你抛落地上，
他还要说他自有他的道理！

LXXVI

The Moving Finger writes; and, having writ,
Moves on: nor all your Piety nor Wit
Shall lure it back to cancel half a Line,
Nor all your Tears wash out a Word of it.

بروی زانوی مشاطه بنشست
چو ساغر بر لب و آئینه بر دست
چو بنشست از خرام آن نخل نوخیز
ز گل شد دامن مشاطه لبریز

指动字成，字成指动；
无论你如何至诚机敏，
也无法反悔抹去半行，
任你洒尽泪水也难洗净。

LXXVII

For let Philosopher and Doctor preach
Of what they will, and what they will not—each
Is but one Link in an eternal Chain
That none can slip, nor break, nor over-reach.

让那些专家学者去絮叨，
他们自以为是的论调吧；
这只不过是无穷极中的一瞬，
既无法摆脱——又不能超越！

LXXVIII

And that inverted Bowl we call The Sky,
Whereunder crawling coop'd we live and die,
Lift not your hands to It for help—for It
As impotently rolls as you or I.

天空是个覆盆，
我们生死其中，
不要俯首向它乞求
它的能力与你我相同。

بوالهوسی بر سر راهی رسید
جلوه‌کنان چارده ماهی بدید
هاله شده گرد قمر معجرش
خیمه زده بر مه و خور چادرش

LXXIX

With Earth's first Clay They did the Last Man knead,
And there of the Last Harvest sow'd the Seed;
And the first Morning of Creation wrote
What the Last Dawn of Reckoning shall read.

第一把土塑出的将是最终的人，
最后的收成便是那最初的种子；
开天辟地的文章
写就的是天地闭合时的声音。

LXXX

Yesterday This Day's Madness did prepare;
To-morrow's Silence, Triumph, or Despair:
Drink! for you know not whence you came, nor why:
Drink! for you know not why you go, nor where.

昨天是今天的颠狂；
今天是明日的沉默、凯旋、绝望：
干吧！你既不知从何来，为何去；
干吧！你又不知因何去，去何方。

LXXXI

I tell you this—when, started from the Goal,
Over the flaming shoulders of the Foal
Of Heav'n Parwin and Mushtari they flung,
In my predestin'd Plot of Dust and Soul.

我告诉你——自诞生起，
他们就把帕尔温①和牟希塔利②
抛过天驹③喷火的肩头，
投入我命定的尘与魂中④⑤。

译注

①帕尔温Parwin，即昴宿Pleiades、牧牛Taurus星座中的一群小星。

②牟希塔利Mushtari，即木星Jupiter。

③天驹，喻太阳。

④此首诗的内容涉及星象学，是占星术的诗艺表达，太阳所在之处，定人吉凶，此乃迷信之语。

⑤原版第4行，在第1、2、4、5版中皆无标点，唯独第3版有一个句号。按意译此诗与下一首可连读。

LXXXII

The Vine had struck a fiber: which about
If clings my Being—let the Dervish flout;
Of my Base metal may be filed a Key,
That shall unlock the Door he howls without.

葡萄生了根：将要与我结缘
让托钵僧①嘲笑吧；
从我这贱躯中铸一把钥匙
可把他咆哮不至的门打开。

译注

①托钵僧（Dervish），苏菲派穆斯林苦行者，自身又有很多分支，核心特征是：培养谦卑之心，乞讨为生。乞之所得分若干份，与其他人分享。他们对奥马尔·哈亚姆又恨又怕，因为他嘲弄了他们的信仰。

LXXXIII

And this I know: whether the one True Light,
Kindle to Love, or Wrath-consume me quite,
One Flash of It within the Tavern caught
Better than in the Temple lost outright.

我知道：无论是欲火燃烧，
还是天怒之火焚我身，
如能在这酒店里看一眼真光，
胜似在神殿里求睹一生。

LXXXIV

What! out of senseless Nothing to provoke
A conscious Something to resent the yoke
Of unpermitted Pleasure, under pain
Of Everlasting Penalties, if broke!

什么！从没知觉的无中
激发出知觉的有
怨恨这禁绝欢乐的桎梏
破除还要遭受惩处！

LXXXV

What! from his helpless Creature be repaid
Pure Gold for what he lent us dross-allay'd—
Sue for a Debt we never did contract,

And cannot answer—Oh the sorry trade!

什么！借破铁烂泥
归还必偿付以纯金——
这是谁订立的规矩，
不平等的黑暗交易！

LXXXVI

Nay, but, for terror of his wrathful Face,
I swear I will not call Injustice Grace;
Not one Good Fellow of the Tavern but
Would kick so poor a Coward from the place.

即使他张开愤怒恐怖的脸，
我发誓我也不会把冤予赐为天恩；
酒馆里又有几个好汉
把这种可怜的懦夫踢出店门。

LXXXVII

Oh Thou, who didst with pitfall and with gin
Beset the Road I was to wander in,
Thou wilt not with Predestin'd Evil round
Enmesh, and then impute my Fall to Sin?

你呀[①]，在我徘徊彷徨的途中
布满美酒和陷阱，

撒下难逃的罪孽罗网
又把堕落的罪名加在我的身上！

译注

①你，指上帝。

LXXXVIII

Oh Thou, who Man of baser Earth didst make,
And ev'n with Paradise devise the Snake:
For all the Sin the Face of wretched Man
Is black with—Man's Forgiveness give—and take!

你呀[①]，你用污泥浊水造人，
设乐园又引入毒蛇[②]；
人的面目被你污以罪孽
你宽恕人，其实你已被人宽恕！

译注

①指上帝。此诗与第81首，同为诅咒上帝之作。

②典出《圣经》创世纪，上帝在伊甸之东建乐园让人类始祖亚当和夏娃居住。但在园中还有一条引夏娃偷吃禁果的蛇。

***

KUZA-NÁMA

酒壶之歌①

译注：

①第1版从第59首至第66首，冠以“KUZA-NÁMA”之名，意为“陶器篇”，第2版从第89首至第97首，与全文用一长条*号线隔开，可视为一组诗；为读者了然，笔者意译为“酒壶之歌”。

LXXXIX①

As under cover of departing Day
Slunk hunger-stricken Ramazán away,
Once more within the Potter's house alone
I stood, surrounded by the Shapes of Clay.

白昼在流逝，趁着夜色
忍饥挨饿的斋月②悄然溜走，
我又独自神游在我的小屋
各种各样的陶器环绕在我的四周③。

译注

①此诗至第90首，第 1 版中冠以“Kuza Nama”之名，意为“陶器篇”，其余各版都与全文隔开，可视为一组诗。

②斋月（Ramazan），伊斯兰教历的九月是信徒们的封斋期，皆清斋断食。斋月从九月见新月那天开始，到下次看到新月结束，斋月，波斯语：Ramazān，英语：Ramadan，阿拉伯语：رمضان رمضان。

③陶人制器的比喻，为外国人常用，参看《圣经·罗马人书》第九章第二十一节。

XC

And once again there gather'd a scarce heard
Whisper among them; as it were, the stirr'd
Ashes of some all but extinguisht Tongue,
Which mine ear kindled into living Word.

它们再次聚首私语
这难以听清的耳语

仿佛消失的灰烬复燃，
从我的耳畔点化为语。

XCI

Said one among them — "Surely not in vain,
My Substance from the common Earth was ta'en,
That He who subtly wrought me into Shape
Should stamp me back to shapeless Earth again."

其中一个说：
“这不过是徒劳
我来自泥土，
必将回归其中。”

XCII

Another said, "Why, ne'er a peevish Boy,
Would break the Cup from which he drank in Joy;
Shall He that of his own free Fancy made
The Vessel, in an after-rage destroy!"

另一个说：“为什么，游手好闲的玩童，
也不会打破他喝的开怀杯，
为爱而作的器皿
怎能在愤怒中摧毁？”

XCIII

None answer'd this; but after silence spake
Some Vessel of a more ungainly Make;
"They sneer at me for leaning all awry;
What! did the Hand then of the Potter shake?"

没有谁回答，沉默片刻
外形古怪的开口：
“世人嘲笑我丑陋：
嗯！难道是因为陶工的手曾颤抖？”

XCIV

Thus with the Dead as with the Living, What?
And Why? so ready, but the Wherefor not,
One on a sudden peevishly exclaim'd,
"Which is the Potter, pray, and which the Pot?"

死者与生者相同，怎么办？
脱口之问？理由令人无语，
一个没好气地突然惊叫，
“哪个是陶工，谁又是陶器？”

XCV

Said one – "Folks of a surly Master tell,

"And daub his Visage with the Smoke of Hell;
"They talk of some sharp Trial of us—Pish!
"He's a Good Fellow, and 'twill all be well."

又一个道："听说主人很粗暴，
"用地狱的烟雾涂抹他的面貌；
"他们说我们经得起严格的测试，呸！
"他是个好人，这决不会错。"

XCVI

"Well," said another, "Whoso will, let try,
"My Clay with long Oblivion is gone dry:
But, fill me with the old familiar Juice,
Methinks I might recover by-and-bye."

"好吧，"另一个默然道："我们试试，
我在长久的忘却中已经干裂；
我只求亲热的酒浆装满我身，
我想我复活将很快。"

XCVII

So while the Vessels one by one were speaking,
One spied the little Crescent all were seeking:
And then they jogg'd each other, "Brother! Brother!
Now for the Porter's shoulder-knot a-creaking? "

陶瓶们纷纷倾谈，

翘望的新月已出斋露面[1]；

他们互相转告："朋友！朋友！

搬酒人的垫肩已吱吱作响！"

译注

①Little moon，意为新月Little cresent moon；伊斯兰教历（阴历）九月封斋，第29天后，如见新月，第二天即开斋，否则便推迟一天。

②陶罐经过搬运人的搬运，进入人世，又能接触到酒浆。

***

XCVIII

Ah, with the Grape my fading Life provide,
And wash my Body whence the Life has died,
And lay me, shrouded in the living Leaf,
By some not unfrequented Garden-side.

哎，我生将谢，请为我准备酒浆，
在我死后，请洗涤我的皮囊，
让落叶轻轻地把我覆盖，
把我埋在没有人迹的花园旁。

XCIX

Whither resorting from the vernal Heat
Shall Old Acquaintance Old Acquaintance greet,
Under the Branch that leans above the Wall
To shed his Blossom over head and feet.

青春的热情已消失不见
老熟人应向老熟人掂念，
墙壁之上的枝丫伸来
落花把我的头脚掩联。

C

Then ev'n my buried Ashes such a snare
Of Vintage shall fling up into the Air,
As not a True-believer passing by
But shall be overtaken unaware;

我的遗体虽然已被埋葬
但它依然在土中哺育葡萄
那硕果累累的卷须
无意间把虔诚之徒缠绕

CI

Indeed the Idols I have loved so long
Have done my credit in Men's Eye much wrong:
Have drown'd my Glory in a shallow Cup,
And sold my Reputation for a Song.

我热爱的这些偶像
令我在世上的眼中蒙羞；
把虚名换成歌声吧，
让光荣消融在杯中。

CII

Indeed, indeed, Repentance oft before
I swore—but was I sober when I swore?
And then and then came Spring. and Rose-in-hand
My thread-bare Penitence apieces tore.

的确，的确，我曾经常忏悔——
但那时我是否清醒？
春风一度，玫瑰在手
我的忏悔又随风飘飞。

CIII

And much as Wine has play'd the Infidel,
And robb'd me of my Robe of Honour—Well,
I often wonder what the Vintners buy
One half so precious as the ware they sell.

尽管酒色背信弃义，
总是剥去我体面的外衣，
但是我常想：有什么
比酒贩卖出的酒更为珍奇。

CIV

Yet Ah, that Spring should vanish with the Rose!
That Youth's sweet-scented manuscript should close!
The Nightingale that in the branches sang,
Ah whence, and whither flown again, who knows!

春天和玫瑰一同消亡！
芬芳的青春手稿也将合上！
夜莺在花枝间娇啼曼唱，
谁能知道她来自何方，又飞向哪里！

CV

Would but the Desert of the Fountain yield
One glimpse—if dimly, yet indeed, reveal'd,
Toward which the fainting Traveller might spring,
As springs the trampled herbage of the field!

沙漠里只要有清泉闪现
即使是模糊迷离，
也令昏迷的行者扑向前去，
犹如被践踏的小草重新挺起。

CVI

Oh if the World were but to re-create,
That we might catch ere closed the Book of Fate,
And make The Writer on a fairer leaf
Inscribe our names, or quite obliterate!

哦，如果世界能够重新创建，
我们在命运之书合上前赶到，
请握笔在洁白的书页上
题写我们的名字，或一笔勾销！

CVII

Better, oh better, cancel from the Scroll
Of Universe one luckless Human Soul,
Than drop by drop enlarge the Flood that rolls
Hoarser with Anguish as the Ages roll.

哦，最好，从宇宙的卷轴中
勾去人世间的这个可怜虫，
让这日积月累的痛苦
如呼啸汹涌的洪波一闪而过。

خلیفه‌زاده هارون الرشید
عمل بهزاد

CVIII

Ah Love! could you and I with Fate conspire
To grasp this sorry Scheme of Things entire,
Would not we shatter it to bits—and then
Re-mould it nearer to the Heart's Desire!

爱！你我他若能同心
把握住这尘世的不幸，
我们就无须把它砸碎
再造一个世界。

ClX

But see! The rising Moon of Heav'n again
Looks for us, Sweet-heart, through the quivering Plane:
How oft hereafter rising will she look
Among those leaves—for one of us in vain!

看！亲爱的，月亮再次升起
通过颤抖的桐叶寻找我们：
以后她将还有多少次升起
在那些叶子中——把我们寻觅！

CX

And when Yourself with silver Foot shall pass
Among the Guests Star-scatter'd on the Grass,
And in your joyous errand reach the spot

گردانیدن وجورپے ادبان بردن
گفت ای یار دست از دامنم بدار که بارها درین مصلحت که تو می‌اندیشی اندیشه کرده‌ام

Where I made One—turn down an empty Glass!

迈着你闪亮的脚
穿梭在草地上寻欢的群客之中，
欣然地走到我曾坐过的地方，
朋友，请为我祭酒一觞！

TAMÁM SHUD

结束

跋

文爱艺

书是有生命的，命运各有不同，《柔波集》的命运尤为奇特——世界上最华贵的书是它，运道最离奇的也是它。

1908年，英国书籍装帧设计名家弗朗西斯·圣高斯基（Francis Sangorski）被大书商亨利·莎乐伦（Henry Sotheran）的热忱感动，为了助他打造一本世界最华丽之书的梦想，花费了几个月的时间构思，用两年的时间才完成了镶满宝石的《柔波集》。这部堪称世界上最奢华的书，在定制之初，莎乐伦要求越奢华越好，但在交货时，他依然被账单吓坏了。此书在1912年伦敦苏富比拍卖会上由纽约商人加布里埃尔·维斯（Gabriel Weis）顺利买走，托运商把它交给首航的泰坦尼克号邮轮运往美国。4月14日，邮轮在大西洋撞上冰山，此书不幸随船上的1500多名乘客葬于海底。更为不幸的是，6周之后，装帧此书的大设计家圣高斯基在苏塞克斯（Sussex）游泳时溺亡。其后不久，圣高斯基作坊里的小师傅一时兴起，照图样又装帧了一部同样的《柔波集》，不巧又遇到第二次世界大战，尽管小师傅把书藏在地窖里，但依然没有躲过德军的轰炸，毁于火海之中。

《柔波集》的译本之多，版本之多，插图之多，设计之华美，装帧之繁复，运道之奇特，无疑是出版史上的奇迹。

我们爱书、写书、出书，只有一个目标：传递思想信息和情感信息——无论书的外在形式如何，只要传递的信息强大，有益于人类，那么无论怎样的命运都无法遏止它的传递。

第5版

第4版

第3版

柔波集

集校版全集

Rubaiyat of Omar Khayyarm

1872年第3版、1879年第4版、1889年第5版

[波斯] 奥马尔·哈亚姆 著
[英] 爱德华·菲茨杰拉德 英译
文爱艺 译

01

清醒吧！太阳已驱散了黑暗，

照亮遁于黑暗中的群星，

阳光之箭把璀璨的光辉

射向苏丹[1]的高瓴。

WAKE! For the Sun who scatter'd into flight

The Stars before him from the Field of Night,

Drives Night along with them from Heav'n, and strikes

The Sultán's Turret with a Shaft of Light.

译注：

1. 苏丹，原文为Sultán，统治者的称号。

02

晨光[1]在幻影降临前消逝，
旅馆[2]里似乎有人呼喊：
“神殿已准备就绪，
参拜人为何依然贪眠？”

Before the phantom of False morning died,
Methought a Voice within the Tavern cried,
"When all the Temple is prepared within,
"Why nods the drowsy Worshipper outside?"

译注：

1 False morning died，即false dawn，天文学称之为zodiacal light（黄道光亮），赤道地区日出日落后一至三小时内因地平线下太阳光经空气中的尘埃团的折射而形成的光；经常与银河同时出现在天上。

2 Tavern解释为inn，小旅馆，与下句Temple对比呼应。

03

此时[1]，公鸡已在啼鸣，在旅馆外面
急切等宿的人们喊道：
“快把门打开，我们只有短暂的休眠，
一旦离去，也许再也不能回还。”

And, as the Cock crew, those who stood before
The Tavern shouted – "Open then the Door!
"You know how little while we have to stay,
And, once departed, may return no more."

译注：

[1] 这句表示承接上首诗。

04

新春[1]复活了旧时的希望，

沉思的灵魂在孤寂中隐藏，

摩西的素手[2]嫁接上它的枝条，

耶稣从此地发出叹息[3]。

Now the New Year reviving old Desires,

The thoughtful Soul to Solitude retires,

Where the WHITE HAND OF MOSES on the Bough

Puts out, and Jesus from the Ground suspires.

译注：

1 古波斯以春分日为元旦，即新春之日。

2 典出《圣经·出埃及记》第四章第六节："耶和华又对他说：'把手放在怀里。'他把手放在怀 里，及至抽出来，不料，手长了大麻风，有雪那样白。"此花似波斯的藏红花。摩西（Moses）：可兰经说摩西手白如雪，故借喻白花。另外，《旧约·出埃及记》第4章的前五节中提到了"摩西的杖（moses's hand），典出《旧约·出埃及记》第4章1—5节。耶和华对摩西说：'你手里是什么？'他说：'是杖。'耶和华说：'丢在地上。'他一丢下去，就变作蛇，摩西便跑开。典喻神迹。"

3 古波斯人认为，耶稣起死回生的法力存在于他的呼吸之中。

05

依兰园[1]的玫瑰消亡无影，

杰木西的七环杯[2]也不知何往；

但葡萄藤里依然流丹绽放，

水畔的鲜花仍旧缤纷遍地。

Iram indeed is gone with all his Rose,

And Jamshyd's Sev'n-ring'd Cup where no one knows;

But still a Ruby kindles in the Vine,

And many a Garden by the Water blows.

译注：

1. 依兰园，原文是Iram，古波斯名园，为夏达德王所建，现已湮没在阿拉伯沙漠之中。
2. 杰木西（Jamshyd），传说中的古波斯王，原意是日之天子，俾什达迪（Pishdadian）王朝的第五世；七环杯为灵杯，象征七天、七海、七行星，为凯克斯鲁（Kaikhosrú）所造，传言得此杯可知去、来、今三世。杯中常盛不死药。古波斯人以七为大，以七为至圣，影响至今。

06

大卫[①]的歌唇紧锁；但是夜莺

用神妙的佩雷微语[②]高歌：

“来！来！来！葡萄美酒啊！”

歌声使玫瑰苍白的脸色红艳。

And David's lips are lockt; but in divine

High-piping Pehlevi, with " Wine! Wine! Wine!

"Red Wine!" – the Nightingale cries to the Rose

That sallow cheek of her's to' incarnadine.

译注：

① 大卫（David），古代善歌者，传说为古希伯来国王，典出《圣经·旧约》。

② 佩雷微语（Péhlevi），3世纪至7世纪期间通行于波斯的语言，属印欧语系之伊朗语族，介于古波斯语与现代波斯语之间。

07

来吧，把酒杯斟满，在春天的火中①
脱去忏悔的冬衣：
时间之鸟②无法永久起飞，
现在它已振翅翱翔。

Come, fill the Cup, and in the fire of Spring
Your Winter garment of Repentance fling:
The Bird of Time has but a little way
To flutter—and the Bird is on the Wing.

译注：

① 中国的春分日，公历（Gregorian Calendar）的3月21日是古波斯传统新年（Nawrūz），新年之前的第一个星期三当晚至第二天天亮，波斯人在街上多次点燃火盆，跳过火盆即可驱走疾病和厄运；此风俗源于公元前6世纪的拜火教（Zoroastrianism）。拜火教由古波斯传入中国后发展为祆教和明教。

② 时间之鸟，指春天之鸟，喻时光如飞。

08

无论在内沙布尔①还是在巴比伦②，

莫问杯中物是苦涩还是香醇，

生活之酒芳香不止，

生命之叶枯荣不息。

Whether at Naishápúr or Babylon,

Whether the Cup with sweet or bitter run,

The Wine of Life keeps oozing drop by drop,

The Leaves of Life keep falling one by one.

译注：

1 内沙布尔（Naishápúr，波斯语：Nīshāpūr），地名，诗人诞生地，位于今伊朗东北部的中呼罗珊省（Razavi Khorasan Province），历史上曾是首府。原是丝绸之路上重要的关口，曾是世界上十大城市之一。13世纪，被蒙古大军攻占。公元1221年，成吉思汗（Ghinggis Khan）的金刀附马脱忽察儿（Toquchar）在此城被冷箭射杀，公主请求成吉思汗屠城。为不留一个活口，托雷（Tolui）下令将所有被杀之人斩首，首级堆成高山，约有170万人被杀。

2 巴比伦（Babylon，波斯语：Bābil），古巴比伦王国及新巴比伦王国的都城，位于幼发拉底河东岸的两河流域中心，现位于伊拉克境内。在伊拉克首都巴格达南部约50公里处。传说中的古代世界七大奇观之一的空中花园，即在此处。

09

你说：朝朝盛开玫瑰，

可哪儿又是昨天玫瑰的下落？

这带来芬芳玫瑰的夏日，

也使杰木西、凯可巴[1]一去不回。

Each Morn a thousand Roses brings, you say:

Yes, but where leaves the Rose of Yesterday?

And this first Summer month that brings the Rose

Shall take Jamshyd and Kaikobád away.

译注：

[1] 凯可巴（Kaikobád），古波斯第二王统（Kaianians）王朝之第一君主。据菲尔多西《列王纪》，凯可巴死后传位长子凯卡乌斯。凯卡乌斯子西亚沃什避难突朗部，入赘驸马，与突朗公主法兰吉斯生一子，即凯霍斯鲁。凯霍斯鲁后回国承继祖父凯卡乌斯之王位。凯为巴列维语尊称，意为首领或统治者，凯扬则是凯之复数。后凯扬演变为世间王者之代称。波斯史中凯扬灵光即指世间人君所享有之神恩与福佑，与中国所谓真命天子意同。

10

消失，随他们消失吧，凯可巴大帝、

凯克斯鲁[1]与我们有什么关系？

让查尔[2]、鲁士[3]恣意咆哮去吧，

哈蒂姆[4]招邀欢筵——也不会叫上你。

Well, let it take them! What have we to do

With Kaikobád the Great, or Kaikhosrú?

Let Zál and Rustum bluster as they will,

Or Hátim call to Supper—heed not you.

译注：

1 凯克斯鲁（Kaihosrú），凯可巴之孙，即波斯帝国的创建者居鲁士（前？一前529），他于前538年占领巴比伦，释放被俘者，灭新巴比伦王国。

2 查尔（Zál），古波斯英雄。原义是白化病；《列王纪》（Shāhnāma，希伯来语：Sefer Melachim，是《旧约圣经》的一部分原文用希伯来语书写）记载，这个白化病婴儿被遗弃山中，被大鹏神鸟（simurgh，大地、海洋和天空的结合体，住在知识之树的树顶，曾亲眼目睹世界的三次大毁灭）发现并养大。

3 鲁士（Rustam），查尔之子，英勇非凡。

4 哈蒂姆（Hátim Tai），公元6世纪阿拉伯塔伊族（Taiy tribe）人。东方贵族，以慷慨著称。

11

请随我踏上这片狭窄之地，

这儿一边是荒原，一边是牧场，

囚奴与国王之名到此消失，

尽管穆罕默德[1]安坐在黄金宝座上。

With me along the strip of Herbage strown

That just divides the desert from the sown,

Where name of Slave and Sultán is forgot—

And Peace to Mahmúd on his golden Throne!

译注:

① 穆罕默德（Máhmúd，979—1030），阿富汗加兹王朝国王，在位期间以极端专制集权，一生长期征战，并多次入侵印度，将国土面积扩大，至今伊朗、阿富汗、巴基斯坦以及印度西北部的广大区域。为10世纪末叶著名的苏丹。

12

树荫下放着诗卷，

一瓶美酒，一个面包，

荒漠中，有你在我身旁欢歌——

噢，荒原，也是天堂！

A Book of Verses underneath the Bough,

A Jug of Wine, a Loaf of Bread – and Thou

Beside me singing in the Wilderness –

Oh, Wilderness were Paradise enow!

13

有人希图现世的荣耀；

有人希图天国的安宁；

噢，且惜今朝，浮名与我何益，

远方的鼓音[1]与我何干！

Some for the Glories of This World; and some

Sigh for the Prophet's Paradise to come;

Ah, take the Cash, and let the Credit go,

Nor heed the rumble of a distant Drum!

译注：

[1] 远方的鼓音：古波斯皇宫外置有大鼓，用于召集军队；暗喻死亡之声。

14

请看盛开的芳香玫瑰，

她说道："我刚含笑绽放尘世，

转瞬我的锦囊便碎裂，

囊中的珍宝只能散落无痕。"

Look to the blowing Rose about us – "Lo,

Laughing," she says, "into the world I blow,

At once the silken tassel of my Purse

Tear, and its Treasure on the Garden throw."

15

节谷如金玉，

挥金如雨泥，

回身如大梦，

墓又被掘启。

And those who husbanded the Golden grain,

And those who flung it to the winds like Rain,

Alike to no such aureate Earth are turn'd

As, buried once, Men want dug up again.

16

人所神往的希求

瞬间云烟成灰；或许经历繁华，然而

如同飘雪覆盖的沙漠，

只闪现一两刻的明辉。

The Worldly Hope men set their Hearts upon

Turns Ashes—or it prospers; and anon,

Like Snow upon the Desert's dusty Face,

Lighting a little hour or two—is gone.

17

天地飘摇逆旅，

昼夜门户交替，

多少荣华富贵，

匆匆而后离去。

Think, in this batter'd Caravanserai

Whose Portals are alternate Night and Day,

How Sultán after Sultán with his Pomp

Abode his destined Hour, and went his way.

18

杰木西豪饮的宫殿[1]
如今是猛狮蜥蜴游弋之地；
巴拉姆国王[2]，
野驴踩过他的头，也惊不醒他的深梦。

They say the Lion and the Lizard keep
The courts where Jamshyd gloried and drank deep:
And Bahrám, that great Hunter—the Wild Ass
Stamps o'er his Head, but cannot break his Sleep.

译注：

1 指现在位于法尔斯省省会色拉子东北面的波斯波利斯。该城又称为塔赫特·伊·杰木西，意为"杰木西的御座"。现在依然存在一些遗迹。

2 巴拉姆（Bahrám），古波斯萨山（Sassanian）王朝（226—642）第14任君主，软弱，好色，曾造七城，涂七色，以七个美女居之，讲七种故事。他在一次捕猎野驴的时候，不小心连人带马栽进山涧。

19

古往今来的玫瑰，

属凯撒[1]葬身处的最红；

曾朵朵招展的玉簪儿[2]，

都根植于美女的尸中。

I sometimes think that never blows so red

The Rose as where some buried Caesar bled;

That every Hyacinth the Garden wears

Dropt in her Lap from some once lovely Head.

译注：

1 凯撒（公元前100—公元前44），古罗马执政官，号称凯撒大帝，被刺身亡。

2 直译为风信子，一种花。风信子（Hyacinthus orientalis），出自古希腊神话：太阳神（Apollo）和西风神（Zephyrus）同时向美少年雅辛托斯（Hyacinth）求爱，雅辛托斯选择了太阳神，嫉妒的西风神将自己的爱人带走，死者从血泊中开出花儿并重生。故风信子有爱情、重生、春天之含义。

20

河畔青青草，

我们枕之眠，

莫要压伤它，

来自美唇边！

And this reviving Herb whose tender Green

Fledges the River-Lip on which we lean—

Ah, lean upon it lightly! for who knows

From what once lovely Lip it springs unseen!

21

噢，我亲爱的，请斟满今日之杯

浇除那昨日之悔和来日之愁，

唉，明天！也许，明天

我已归入尘土[①]。

Ah, my Belovéd, fill the Cup that clears

TO-DAY of past Regrets and future Fears:

To-morrow! — Why, To-morrow I may be

Myself with Yesterday's Sev'n thousand Years.

译注：

① 原文意为“归入昨日的七千岁”，古波斯人认为地球的年龄为七千年，此处引申意为人死后归于尘土，故译为“我已归入尘土”。法文译者尼古拉认为，七千年是指亚当创造人类至今的时间。

22

我们所钟爱的人间之美，

时光把它从葡萄中榨成酒浆，

我们从中仅饮得三杯两盏，

瞬间即无声无息地永久长眠。

For some we loved, the loveliest and the best

That from his Vintage rolling Time hath prest,

Have drunk their Cup a Round or two before,

And one by one crept silently to rest.

23

秾芳盛满了古人的华堂，

他们走了，我们尽情地在此盛装欢畅，

我们也将入土长眠，

接下来——又是谁在我们的上面狂欢？

And we, that now make merry in the Room

They left, and Summer dresses in new bloom,

Ourselves must we beneath the Couch of Earth

Descend—ourselves to make a Couch—for whom?

24

哎，趁我们入土之前，

尽情地享受人间；

有朝一日，尘归尘，土归土，

歌声美酒，永远也不能同眠！

Ah, make the most of what we yet may spend,

Before we too into the Dust descend;

Dust into Dust, and under Dust to lie,

Sans[①] Wine, sans Song, sans Singer, and—sans End!

译注：

① Sans，源自法文的古英语，意为：without。

25

有人终日奔波忙碌，

有人乞求来生成就，

敲钟人[1]从黑暗之塔[2]中呼喊：

“蠢人！报偿无处可求。”

Alike for those who for TO-DAY prepare,
And those that after some TO-MORROW stare,
A Muezzín from the Tower of Darkness cries,
"Fools! your Reward is neither Here nor There."

译注：

1 原文是Muezzín，意为清真寺塔楼上的守钟人，每天在指定的时刻敲钟叫信徒们祈祷。

2 黑暗之塔，喻不可知的命运。

26

自古高谈阔论的圣贤，

惯会说古论今，

一旦口被尘封，只会自嘲声声，

同江湖预言者没有两样。

Why, all the Saints and Sages who discuss'd
Of the Two Worlds so wisely—they are thrust
Like foolish Prophets forth; their Words to Scorn
Are scatter'd, and their Mouths are stopt with Dust.

27

青春时分，我曾热切地

拜访名流圣人，倾听谈生论死的

高论；但我返归时

依然只能原路走回。

Myself when young did eagerly frequent

Doctor and Saint, and heard great argument

About it and about: but evermore

Came out by the same door where in I went.

28

我学会了播种智慧，

并亲手培植它吐穗；

而今收获的却只有：

“来如流水，逝如风吹。”[1]

With them the seed of Wisdom did I sow,
And with mine own hand wrought to make it grow;
And this was all the Harvest that I reap'd—
"I came like Water, and like Wind I go."

译注：

[1] 意为“我正在风的手中消逝”。古波斯诗人法里德·阿尔-丁·阿塔尔（Farid od-Din Attar，约1142—约1220）记载莫尔克被杀时吟叹此句。

29

飘然入世，如水不由自主，

不知为何来，亦不知来自何处；

飘然出世，如风不能停留，

吹过沙丘，亦不知飘向哪里。

Into this Universe, and Why not knowing

Nor Whence, like Water willy-nilly flowing;

And out of it, as Wind along the Waste,

I know not Whither, willy-nilly blowing.

30

莫问何处来，

莫问哪里去！

狂欢饮禁酒，

淹没此记忆！

What, without asking, hither hurried Whence?

And, without asking, Whither hurried hence!

Oh, many a Cup of this forbidden Wine

Must drown the memory of that insolence!

31

从大地的心中腾空而起，

飞过七重天坐上土星高椅[1]，

沿途巧解无数难破之谜；

但人生这个谜却总也猜不透。

Up from Earth's Centre through the Seventh Gate

I rose, and on the Throne of Saturn sate,

And many a Knot unravel'd by the Road;

But not the Master-knot of Human Fate.

译注：

[1] hurried，土星，波斯神话中，视土星为第七重天的主宰。西方人古代称为Saturnus（拉丁文），为太阳系八大行星之一。土星具有美丽的环带结构，截止2012年已发现62颗卫星，离地球最远。古代中国称为镇星或填星。

32

门紧锁，我找不到钥匙，

帷幕紧，我看不到内幕；

仔细听，你我被人指点，

不多时，你我都将消失。

There was the Door to which I found no Key;

There was the Veil through which I might not see:

Some little talk awhile of ME and THEE

There was — and then no more of THEE and ME[1].

译注：

[1] 我（ME）指个体的存在，你（THEE）指芸芸众生。

33

大地无言；紫波的大海亦无言[1]

翻卷着被遗弃的哀痛；

滚滚太空，它的十二星辰

日吞夜吐，但依然无言。

Earth could not answer; nor the Seas that mourn

In flowing Purple, of their Lord Forlorn;

Nor rolling Heaven, with all his Signs reveal'd

And hidden by the sleeve of Night and Morn.

译注：

[1]1856年人工合成苯胺紫（methyl violet）染料之前，紫色在全球范围内极难获得。皇家紫色的原料，来自地中海海螺（Haustellum brandaris）的分泌物。提炼一克这种染料，大约需要一万枚海螺的分泌物，所以紫色是欧洲和西亚皇室袍服的专用颜色，称之为皇家紫色（Royal purle）。紫色是血液干涸之色，故含有高贵、尊严、牺牲之义。

34

叩问我的神灵，

请它为我照明；

只听空谷传音，

其实我是盲瞽！

Then of the THEE IN ME who works behind

The Veil, I lifted up my hands to find

A Lamp amid the Darkness; and I heard,

As from Without—"THE ME WITHIN THEE BLIND!"

35

俯就在酒的唇边，

想探究生之奥秘：

两唇相吻，酒唇低语，

“快快畅饮，死后难聚”。

Then to the Lip of this poor earthen Urn

I lean'd, the Secret of my Life to learn:

And Lip to Lip it murmur'd—"While you live,

"Drink!—for, once dead, you never shall return."

36

幽幽低语的这个酒杯[1]

曾经鲜活痛饮在人间；

哎！而今我吻着它的唇，

不知它曾接受过多少回！

I think the Vessel, that with fugitive

Articulation answer'd, once did live,

And drink; and Ah! the passive Lip I kiss'd,

How many Kisses might it take—and give!

译注：

[1] 古波斯诗人法里德·阿尔-丁·阿塔尔（Farid od-Din Attar，约1142—约1220）在诗中写道：旅人用双手托起泉水喝，甘甜，当他用路人留下的陶罐来饮，同样的水却饮出了苦味。来自天空的声音告诉他，现在的陶土，曾经也是鲜活的生命，万物流转，当人化为尘土，制为容器，仍无法消弭残留于土中的苦涩。

37

我曾经在路途中
看见陶工用力捣土，
陶土用它从未开启的舌传出微弱的
哀号——“轻点，兄弟，轻点，求你！”

For I remember stopping by the way
To watch a Potter thumping his wet Clay:
And with its all-obliterated Tongue
It murmur'd — "Gently, Brother, gently, pray!"

38

我们来自泥土，
又归于泥土，
代代如此，
这难道仅是传言？

And has not such a Story from of Old
Down Man's successive generations roll'd
Of such a clod of saturated Earth
Cast by the Maker into Human mould?

39

我们从杯中奠洒美酒，
一点一滴潜入地底深处，
渗进逝者难瞑的双目，
消除它焦灼无解的痛苦。

And not a drop that from our Cups we throw
For Earth to drink of, but may steal below
To quench the fire of Anguish in some Eye
There hidden—far beneath, and long ago.

40

郁金香从土中仰起，

把晨露如琼浆般承受，

你也该如此举杯，

直到天地将你逆转——一如倾倒酒杯。

As then the Tulip for her morning sup

Of Heav'nly Vintage from the soil looks up,

Do you devoutly do the like, till Heav'n

To Earth invert you—like an empty Cup.

41

别再为天上人间烦闷，
明朝的纷繁让风处理，
酒神的长发软如松丝，
请用你的手为它梳理。

Perplext no more with Human or Divine,
To-morrow's tangle to the winds resign,
And lose your fingers in the tresses of
The Cypress[①]-slender Minister of Wine.

译注：

① cypress，柏属植物（原产北美、欧、亚），柏树；柏树枝（用作哀悼的标志）；似柏树树种；此处专指柏木属植物，俗名cypress of shirāz，树高达35米，圆锥形狭长树冠，树冠下缘宽度一般不到总树高的十分之一，气味芳馥。波斯文学中常用来形容女性身躯的亭亭玉立和雄健挺拔的男性气味芳馥。波斯文学中常用来形容女性身躯的亭亭玉立和雄健挺拔男性的身躯，含有“高贵”“自由”之意，树的叶子被用来形容人的头发。

42

如果说美酒和美唇，

都将归入梦境；

你是否知道今日即是昨天，

明朝也是如此。

And if the Wine you drink, the Lip you press,

End in what All begins and ends in—Yes;

Think then you are TO-DAY what YESTERDAY

You were—TO-MORROW you shall not be less.

43

如果在酒岸
巧遇酒乡天使，
他邀你举杯
你千万别犹豫。

So when the Angel of the darker Drink
At last shall find you by the river-brink,
And, offering his Cup, invite your Soul
Forth to your Lips to quaff—you shall not shrink.

44

如果灵魂能抛弃躯体，

赤裸地遨游天地，

那它为什么还要停在其中，

难道它不感到躯体的丑陋？

Why, if the Soul can fling the Dust aside,

And naked on the Air of Heaven ride,

Wer't not a Shame—wer't not a Shame for him

In this clay carcase crippled to abide?

45

这个只能小憩一时的天幕，

在苏丹奔赴冥国时开启；

黑暗的命运[1]很快关闭，

静待下一位起息。

'Tis but a Tent where takes his one day's rest

A Sultán to the realm of Death addrest;

The Sultán rises, and the dark Ferrásh

Strikes, and prepares it for another Guest.

译注：

1 原文是Ferrásh，本意为开启天幕者，此处引申意为造化、命运。

46

虽然我们不存在了，

但生命之火依然；

我们不过是酒中的一滴，

永恒的造化[1]将不停地斟酌。

And fear not lest Existence closing your

Account, and mine, should know the like no more;

The Eternal Sáki from that Bowl has pour'd

Millions of Bubbles like us, and will pour.

译注：

[1] 原文是Sáki，波斯语，原意为托杯斟酒者，引申义为造化。

47

当你我消失之后，

时间依然如故，

你我的来去——

犹如小石子投入海中。

When You and I behind the Veil are past,
Oh, but the long, long while the World shall last,
Which of our Coming and Departure heeds
As the Sea's self should heed a pebble-cast.

48

片刻的停留——这瞬间的滋味
细品这荒漠甘泉的生命之水
看！幻影商队已从无中来
又归无中去——噢，快饮吧！

A Moment's Halt—a momentary taste
Of BEING from the Well amid the Waste—
And Lo!—the phantom Caravan has reach'd
The NOTHING it set out from—Oh, make haste!

49

如果你愿意花宝贵的光阴

去探寻人生——朋友，那就去吧！

真理和谬误一线之别，

舍此，生活有何凭依？

Would you that spangle of Existence spend

About THE SECRET – quick about it, Friend!

A Hair perhaps divides the False and True –

And upon what, prithee, may life depend?

50

真理和谬误一线之隔；

是的；只一个“阿里夫”[1]便至达——

只要你能领悟——

它便引领你皈依真主；

A Hair perhaps divides the False and True;

Yes; and a single Alif were the clue—

Could you but find it—to the Treasure-house,

And peradventure to THE MASTER too;

译注：

[1] 阿里夫，原文是（Alif），阿拉伯字母中的第一个字母，波斯语中发音为（Alef）；伊斯兰教中的真主安拉（Alllah）也以此为字首。印度教梵文经本《薄伽梵歌》(Bhagavad Gītā；英译：Song of God，汉语意译：神之歌、主黑天之歌；薄伽梵歌的字面意思是“主之歌”或“神之歌”，这里的主或者神就是黑天，薄伽梵相当于上帝，梵相当于圣灵：“我是所有文字的A字母，我是离合释中的相违释。我是流逝无尽中的永恒，我是面向一切的创造者。”

51

他看似无形，却无处不在，

如水银般流动，消除你的痛疼；

赋形于万物，从月至鱼[1]，

都在变化中消亡；而他永存；

Whose secret Presence, through Creation's veins

Running Quicksilver-like eludes your pains;

Taking all shapes from Máh to Máhi and

They change and perish all—but He remains;

译注：

1 古波斯神话，万物始于月而终于鱼。另一说为：我们生活的世界是几经周折背负于鱼背之上的。故古波斯文az māh māhī（从鱼到月），鱼借指大地，月代指天空，喻指世界“从大地到天空”“从低处到高处”。

52

瞬即闪现瞬即消散，

人生如戏黑暗迷茫，

各自登场各自观赏，

戏如人生终归散场。

A moment guessed—then back behind the Fold

Immerst of Darkness round the Drama roll'd

Which, for the Pastime of Eternity,

He doth Himself contrive, enact, behold.

53

在这无情的大地上，
那重门紧闭的天堂，
今日的你，还可凝视，
明日的你又将怎样？

But if in vain, down on the stubborn floor
Of Earth, and up to Heav'n's unopening Door,
You gaze TO-DAY, while You are You—how then
TO-MORROW, when You shall be You no more?

54

别浪费光阴，

莫追求虚空；

一杯美酒在手，

何必空自担忧。

Waste not your Hour, nor in the vain pursuit

Of This and That endeavour and dispute;

Better be jocund with the fruitful Grape

Than sadden after none, or bitter, Fruit.

55

你知道，我的朋友，

我在家中举行盛宴；

我休了不孕的理性，

迎来葡萄的女儿[①]做我的新娘。

You know, my Friends, with what a brave Carouse

I made a Second Marriage in my house;

Divorced old barren Reason from my Bed,

And took the Daughter of the Vine to Spouse.

译注：

① 葡萄的女儿，喻指葡萄酒。

56

虽然可以按几何原理判断正误，

虽然可以按逻辑区分兴衰荣辱，

但在人欲探究的一切中，

除酒之外我一无所获。

For "IS" and "IS-NOT" though with Rule and Line

And "UP-AND-DOWN" by Logic I define,

Of all that one should care to fathom, I

was never deep in anything but — Wine.

57

唉，人们说我的推算高明，

我真的重排了岁月吗？

我只不过是从历史中

勾销了未生的明天和死去的昨天。

Ah, but my Computations, People say,

Reduced the Year to better reckoning?—Nay,

'Twas only striking from the Calendar

Unborn To-morrow and dead Yesterday.

58

不久前，在酒店门口，

暮色中走来一位天使，

肩上扛着土瓶，他让我品尝

瓶中之物——原来是葡萄美酒！

And lately, by the Tavern Door agape,

Came shining through the Dusk an Angel Shape

Bearing a Vessel on his Shoulder; and

He bid me taste of it; and 'twas—the Grape!

59

葡萄美酒，你以绝对的辩才

令纷争的教派[1]哑口无言；

你是至尊的炼金师，

瞬间把生活之铅点化成金。

The Grape that can with Logic absolute

The Two-and-Seventy jarring Sects confute:

The sovereign Alchemist that in a trice

Life's leaden metal into Gold transmute;

译注：

1 伊斯兰教传统说法，伊斯兰之教派分裂为七十三派，其中七十二派会下火狱，只有一派进乐园。

60

你是崇高的至圣穆罕默德，

你驱除一切妖魔鬼怪，

那入侵鬼魂的悲伤恐惧

在你的利剑下都纷纷逃窜。

The mighty Mahmúd, Allah-breathing Lord,

That all the misbelieving and black Horde

Of Fears and Sorrows that infest the Soul

Scatters before him with his whirlwind Sword.

61

如果是上帝酿造此美酒，

谁敢把缠绕的卷须[1]咒成陷阱？

天赐之福，难道我们不应该享用？

是灾祸——那么谁是祸手？

Why, be this Juice the growth of God, who dare

Blaspheme the twisted tendril as a Snare?

A Blessing, we should use it, should we not?

And if a Curse—why, then, Who set it there?

译注：

1 卷须，植物学名词，植物用来缠绕或附着其他物体的器官，此处指葡萄卷须。

62

如果害怕来世报应[1]，

或者被来世的神妙迷惑，

我一定断掉此杯，

但要等我死了以后！

I must abjure the Balm of Life, I must,

Scared by some After-reckoning ta'en on trust,

Or lured with Hope of some Diviner Drink,

To fill the Cup—when crumbled into Dust!

译注：

[1] 来世报应，回教认为今世禁欲，来世得入天堂，有美女和醇酒为伴，反之则下地狱。

63

哎！无论是天堂还是地狱，

只有一事无疑——此生如飞，

余者皆是谎言；

花开之后，便是永远的凋亡。

Oh threats of Hell and Hopes of Paradise!

One thing at least is certain – This Life flies;

One thing is certain and the rest is Lies;

The Flower that once has blown for ever dies.

64

奇怪，真是奇怪——

不计其数的死者，

却无一人归来，

告知我们该走的路。

Strange, is it not? that of the myriads who

Before us pass'd the door of Darkness through,

Not one returns to tell us of the Road,

Which to discover we must travel too.

65

先贤圣哲的宣教
不过是痴人说梦，
醒后告别了同伴
匆匆又归梦中。

The Revelations of Devout and Learn'd
Who rose before us, and as Prophets burn'd,
Are all but Stories, which, awoke from Sleep
They told their comrades, and to Sleep return'd.

66

我把我的灵魂送入幽冥之境，

去翻阅我死后的片言只语；

我的灵魂归来告知：

“我自己便是天堂和地狱！”

I sent my Soul through the Invisible,

Some letter of that After-life to spell:

And by and by my Soul return'd to me,

And answer'd "I Myself am Heav'n and Hell:"

67

天堂是奢望的幻影，

地狱是欲望的虚像，

我们从欲望中现身，

不久将从此处忘形。

Heav'n but the Vision of fulfill'd Desire,

And Hell the Shadow from a Soul on fire,

Cast on the Darkness into which Ourselves,

So late emerged from, shall so soon expire.

68

我们不过是一群幻影，

绕着灯来去匆匆，

在深更夜半

点燃，在魔术师的手中。

We are no other than a moving row

Of Magic Shadow-shapes that come and go

Round with the Sun-illumined Lantern held

In Midnight by the Master of the Show;

69

我们不过是一群可怜的棋子
在昼与夜的棋盘上布局；
任它如何纵横拼杀，
最终都将归于匣中长眠。

But helpless Pieces of the Game He plays
Upon this Chequer-board of Nights and Days;
Hither and thither moves, and checks, and slays,
And one by one back in the Closet lays.

70

球只能唯命是从，

一任击打者随意抛弄；

把你抛落地上，

他还要说他自有他的道理！

The Ball no question makes of Ayes and Noes,

But Here or There as strikes the Player goes;

And He that toss'd you down into the Field,

He knows about it all—HE knows—HE knows!

71

指动字成，字成指动；

无论你如何至诚机敏，

也无法反悔抹去半行，

任你洒尽泪水也难洗净。

The Moving Finger writes; and, having writ,

Moves on: nor all your Piety nor Wit

Shall lure it back to cancel half a Line,

Nor all your Tears wash out a Word of it.

72

天空是个覆盆，

我们生死其中，

不要俯首向它乞求

它的能力与你我相同。

And that inverted Bowl they call the Sky,

Whereunder crawling coop'd we live and die,

Lift not your hands to It for help—for It

As impotently moves as you or I.

73

第一把土塑出的将是最终的人，

最后的收成便是那最初的种子；

开天辟地的文章

写就的是天地闭合时的声音。

With Earth's first Clay They did the Last Man knead,

And there of the Last Harvest sow'd the Seed:

And the first Morning of Creation wrote

What the Last Dawn of Reckoning shall read.

74

昨天是今天的颠狂；

今天是明日的沉默、凯旋、绝望：

痛饮吧！你既不知从何来，为何去；

痛饮吧！你又不知因何去，去何方。

YESTERDAY This Day's Madness did prepare;

TO-MORROW's Silence, Triumph, or Despair:

Drink! for you not know whence you came, nor why:

Drink! for you know not why you go, nor where.

75

我告诉你——自诞生起，

他们就把帕尔温[1]和牟希塔利[2]

抛过天驹[3]喷火的肩头，

投入我命定的尘与魂中[4][5]。

I tell you this—When, started from the Goal,

Over the flaming shoulders of the Foal

Of Heav'n Parwin and Mushtarí they flung,

In my predestined Plot of Dust and Soul.

译注：

1 帕尔温（Parwin），即昴宿（Pleiades）、金牛（Taurus）星座中的一群小星。

2 牟希塔利（Mushtarí），即木星（Jupiter）。

3 天驹，喻太阳。

4 此诗的内容涉及星象学，是占星术的诗艺表达，太阳所在处，定人吉凶，此乃迷信之语。

5 原版第４行，在第1、2、4、5版中皆无标点，唯独第3版有一个句号。按意译此诗与下一首可连读。

76

葡萄生了根，将要与我结缘——

让托钵僧[1]嘲笑吧；

从我这贱躯中铸一把钥匙

可把他咆哮不至的门打开。

The Vine had struck a fiber: which about

It clings my Being—let the Dervish flout;

Of my Base metal may be filed a Key

That shall unlock the Door he howls without.

译注：

1 托钵僧（Dervish），苏菲派穆斯林苦行者，自身又有很多分支，核心特征是：培养谦卑之心，乞讨为生。乞之所得分若干份，与其他人分享。他们对奥马尔·哈亚姆又恨又怕，因为他嘲弄了他们的信仰。

77

我知道：无论是欲火燃烧，

还是天怒之火焚我身，

如能在这酒店里看一眼真光，

胜似在神殿里求睹一生。

And this I know: whether the one True Light

Kindle to Love, or Wrath-consume me quite,

One Flash of It within the Tavern caught

Better than in the Temple lost outright.

78

什么！从没知觉的无中

激发出知觉的有，

怨恨这禁绝欢乐的桎梏，

破除还要遭受惩处！

What! out of senseless Nothing to provoke
A conscious Something to resent the yoke
Of unpermitted Pleasure, under pain
Of Everlasting Penalties, if broke!

79

什么！借破铁烂泥，

归还必偿付以纯金——

这是谁订立的规矩？

不平等的黑暗交易！

What! from his helpless Creature be repaid

Pure Gold for what he lent him dross-allay'd—

Sue for a Debt we never did contract,

And cannot answer—Oh the sorry trade!

80

你呀[1]，在我徘徊彷徨的途中

布满美酒和陷阱，

撒下难逃的罪孽罗网，

又把堕落的罪名加在我的身上！

Oh Thou, who didst with pitfall and with gin

Beset the Road I was to wander in,

Thou wilt not with Predestined Evil round

Enmesh, and then impute my Fall to Sin!

译注：

1 你，指上帝。

81

你呀[1]，你用污泥浊水造人，

设乐园又引入毒蛇[2]；

人的面目被你污以罪孽，

你宽恕人，其实你已被人宽恕！

Oh Thou, who Man of baser Earth didst make,

And ev'n with Paradise devise the Snake:

For all the Sin wherewith the Face of Man

Is blacken'd—Man's forgiveness give—and take!

译注：

1 指上帝。此诗与第80首同为诅咒上帝之作。

2 典出《圣经 · 创世纪》，上帝在伊甸之东建乐园让人类始祖亚当和夏娃居住。但在园中还有一条引夏娃偷吃禁果的蛇。

82 [1]

白昼在流逝，趁着夜色，
忍饥挨饿的斋月[2]悄然溜走，
我又独自神游在我的小屋，
各种各样的陶器环绕在我的四周[3]。

As under cover of departing Day
Slunk hunger-stricken Ramazán away,
Once more within the Potter's house alone
I stood, surrounded by the Shapes of Clay.

译注：

1. 此诗至第90首，第1版中冠以“Kuza Nama”之名，意为“陶器篇”，其余各版都与全文隔开，可视为一组诗。
2. 斋月（Ramazán），伊斯兰教历的九月是信徒们的封斋期，皆清斋断食。斋月从九月见新月那天开始，到下次看到新月结束，斋月，波斯语：Ramazān,英语：Ramadan，阿拉伯语：رمضان) رمضان 。
3. 陶人制器的比喻，为外国人常用，参看《圣经·罗马人书》第九章第二十一节。

83

那形状姿态万千，
大大小小站立一旁；
有的像是在倾诉，
另一些仿佛在聆听。

Shapes of all Sorts and Sizes, great and small,
That stood along the floor and by the wall;
And some loquacious Vessels were; and some
Listen'd perhaps, but never talk'd at all.

84

其中一个说：

“这不是徒劳，

我来自泥土，

将回归其中。”

Said one among them — "Surely not in vain

My substance of the common Earth was ta'en

And to this Figure molded, to be broke,

Or trampled back to shapeless Earth again."

85

接着第二个说：

“没人会砸碎欢饮的茶杯；

亲手制作的器皿

不会在怒火中破损。”

Then said a Second — "Ne'er a peevish Boy

Would break the Bowl from which he drank in joy;

And He that with his hand the Vessel made

Will surely not in after Wrath destroy."

86

沉默片刻，

外形古怪的开口：

“世人嘲笑我丑陋——

嗯！难道是因为陶工的手曾颤抖？”

After a momentary silence spake

Some Vessel of a more ungainly Make;

"They sneer at me for leaning all awry:

What! did the Hand then of the Potter shake?"

87

听此言，泛神论[1]的小瓶
生气道：
“什么陶工陶器，我问你，
谁是陶工，谁又是陶器？”

Whereat some one of the loquacious Lot—
I think a Súfi pipkin—waxing hot—
"All this of Pot and Potter—Tell me then,
Who is the Potter, pray, and who the Pot?"

译注：

[1] 泛神论（Safi），古波斯学派之一，后与伊斯兰教融合成伊斯兰苏菲派。标志特征是苦行、禁欲与神秘。

88

又一个道："你们胡言乱语，

我主会把你们投入地狱，

打碎你们这些倒霉的家伙！

这决不会错。"

"Why," said another, "Some there are who tell

Of one who threatens he will toss to Hell

The luckless Pots he marr'd in making—Pish!

He's a Good Fellow, and 't will all be well."

89

另一个默然道："管它谁做谁买，
我在长久的忘却中已经干裂；
我只求亲热的酒浆装满我身，
我想我很快就会复活。"

"Well," murmur'd one, "Let whoso make or buy,
My Clay with long Oblivion is gone dry:
But fill me with the old familiar Juice,
Methinks I might recover by and by."

90

陶瓶们纷纷倾谈，

翘望的新月已出斋露面①；

他们互相转告：“朋友！朋友！

搬酒人的垫肩已吱吱作响！”②

So while the Vessels one by one were speaking,

The little Moon look'd in that all were seeking:

And then they jogg'd each other, "Brother! Brother!

Now for the Porter's shoulders' knot a-creaking!"

译注：

① Little moon,意为新月Little cresent moon；伊斯兰教历（阴历）九月封斋，第29天后，如见新月，第二天即开斋，否则便推迟一天。

② 陶罐经过搬运人的搬运，进入人世，又能接触到酒浆。

91

哎，我生将谢，请为我准备酒浆，

在我死后，请洗涤我的皮囊，

让落叶轻轻地把我覆盖，

把我埋在没有人迹的花园旁。

Ah, with the Grape my fading Life provide,

And wash the Body whence the Life has died,

And lay me, shrouded in the living Leaf,

By some not unfrequented Garden-side.

92

我的遗体虽然已被埋葬，

但它依然在土中哺育葡萄，

那硕果累累的卷须

无意间把虔诚之徒缠绕。

That ev'n my buried Ashes such a snare

Of Vintage shall fling up into the Air

As not a True-believer passing by

But shall be overtaken unaware.

93

我热爱的这些偶像

令我在世上蒙羞；

把虚名换成歌声吧，

让光荣消融在杯中。

Indeed the Idols I have loved so long

Have done my credit in this World much wrong:

Have drown'd my Glory in a shallow Cup,

And sold my Reputation for a Song.

94

的确，的确，我曾经常忏悔——

但那时我是否清醒？

春风一度，玫瑰在手，

我的忏悔又随风飘飞。

Indeed, indeed, Repentance oft before
I swore — but was I sober when I swore?
And then and then came Spring, and Rose-in-hand
My thread-bare Penitence apieces tore.

95

尽管酒色背信弃义，

总是剥去我体面的外衣，

但是我常想：有什么

比酒贩卖出的酒更为珍奇？

And much as Wine has play'd the Infidel,
And robb'd me of my Robe of Honour—Well,
I wonder often what the Vintners buy
One half so precious as the stuff they sell.

96

春天和玫瑰一同消亡！

芬芳的青春手稿也将合上！

夜莺在花枝间娇啼曼唱，

谁能知道她来自哪里，又飞向何方！

Yet Ah, that Spring should vanish with the Rose!

That Youth's sweet-scented manuscript should close!

The Nightingale that in the branches sang,

Ah whence, and whither flown again, who knows!

97

沙漠里只要有清泉闪现，
即使是模糊迷离，
也令昏迷的行者扑向前去，
犹如被践踏的小草重新挺起。

Would but the Desert of the Fountain yield
One glimpse—if dimly, yet indeed, reveal'd,
To which the fainting Traveller might spring,
As springs the trampled herbage of the field!

98

但愿天使及早飞来,

停止这刚开启的命运之书，

令那严厉的书写者重新开笔,

否则，就让他全盘抹去！

Would but some wingéd Angel ere too late

Arrest the yet unfolded Roll of Fate,

And make the stern Recorder otherwise

Enregister, or quite obliterate!

99

爱！你我他若能同心
把握住这尘世的不幸，
我们就无须把它砸碎
再造一个世界！

Ah Love! could you and I with Him conspire
To grasp this sorry Scheme of Things entire,
Would not we shatter it to bits—and then
Re-mold it nearer to the Heart's Desire!

100

窥人的明月又升起了——
你将还要经历多少回阴晴圆缺；
当你再光临此园时，
恐怕有人已再难寻觅！

Yon rising Moon that looks for us again –
How oft hereafter will she wax and wane;
How oft hereafter rising look for us
Through this same Garden-and for one in vain!

101

如果你也像这月儿
穿梭在草地上寻欢的群客之中，
欣然地走到我曾坐过的地方，
朋友，请为我祭酒一觞！

And when like her, oh Sákí, you shall pass
Among the Guests Star-scatter'd on the Grass,
And in your joyous errand reach the spot
Where I made One—turn down an empty Glass!

TAMÁM SHUD

结束

译注：

TAMÁM SHUD，结束，即 It is ended 。

《柔波集》版本对照表

COMPARATIVE TABLE OF STANZAS IN THE FIVE EDITIONS

Ed.1	Ed.2	Edd.3,4&5
Preface	LXIX	XLIV
Preface	LXX	XLV
I	I	I
II	II	II
III	III	III
IV	IV	IV
V	V	V
VI	VI	VI
VII	VII	VII
VIII	IX	IX
IX	X	X
X	XI	XI
XI	XII	XII
XII	XIII	XIII
XIII	XV	XIV
XIV	XVII	XVI

XV	XVI	XV
XVI	XVIII	XVII
XVII	XIX	XVIII
XVIII	XXIV	XIX
XIX	XXV	XX
XX	XXI	XXI
XXI	XXII	XXII
XXII	XXIII	XXIII
XXIII	XXVI	XXIV
XXIV	XXVII	XXV
XXV	XXIX	XXVI
XXVI	LXVI	LXIII
XXVII	XXX	XXVII
XXVIII	XXXI	XXVIII
XXIX	XXXII	XXIX
XXX	XXXIII	XXX
XXXI	XXXIV	XXXI
XXXII	XXXV	XXXII
XXXIII	XXXVII	XXXIV
XXXIV	XXXVIII	XXXV

XXXV	XXXIX	XXXVI
XXXVI	XL	XXXVII
XXXVII		
XXXVIII	XLIX	XLVIII
XXXIX	LVI	LIV
XL	LVII	LV
XLI	LVIII	LVI
XLII	LX	LVIII
XLIII	LXI	LIX
XLIV	LXII	LX
XLV		
XLVI	LXXIII	LXVIII
XLVII	XLV	XLII
XLVIII	XLVI	XLIII
XLIX	LXXIV	LXIX
L	LXXV	LXX
LI	LXXVI	LXXI
LII	LXXVIII	LXXII
LIII	LXXIX	LXXIII
LIV	LXXXI	LXXV

LV
LVI
LVII
LVIII
LIX
LX
LXI
LXII
LXIII
LXIV
LXV
LXVI
LXVII
LXVIII
LXIX
LXX
LXXI
LXXII
LXXIII
LXXIV

LXXXII
LXXXIII
LXXXVII
LXXXVIII
LXXXIX
XCIV
XCI
XCII
XCIII
XCV
XCVI
XCVII
XCVIII
C
CI
CII
CIII
CIV
CVIII
CIX

LXXVI
LXXVII
LXXX
LXXXI
LXXXII
LXXXVII
LXXXIV
LXXXV
LXXXVI
LXXXVIII
LXXXIX
XC
XCI
XCII
XCIII
XCIV
XCV
XCVI
XCIX
C

LXXV	CX	CI
	VIII	VIII
		XIV
	XX	Note on XVIII
	XXVIII	
	XXXVI	XXXIII
	XLI	XXXVIII
	XLII	XXXIX
	XLIII	XL
	XLIV	
	XLVII	XLVI
	XLVIII	XLVII
	L	XLIX
	LI	L
	LII	LI
	LIII	LII
	LIV	LIII
	LV	XLI
	LIX	LVII
	LXIII	LXI

LXIV	LXII
LXV	
LXVII	LXIV
LXVIII	LXV
LXIX	XLIV
LXX	XLV
LXXI	LXVI
LXXII	LXVII
LXXVII	
LXXX	LXXIV
LXXXIV	LXXVIII
LXXXV	LXXIX
LXXXVI	
XC	LXXXIII
XCIX	
CV	XCVII
CVI	XCVIII
CVII	

《柔波集》版本对照表

爱德华·菲茨杰拉德英译的《柔波集》初版于 1859 年，收诗 75 首。1868 年增订重编了第二版，增至 110 首。1872 年修订出版了第三版；1879 年再次修订出版了第四版；1889 年修正的第五版，都是 101 首。

详情列表如下：

第一版	第二版	第三、四、五版
1	1	1
2	2	2
3	3	3
4	4	4
5	5	5
6	6	6
7	7	7
8	9	9
9	10	10
10	11	11
11	12	12
12	13	13
13	15	14
14	17	16
15	16	15
16	18	17
17	1	18
18	24	19

第一版	第二版	第三、四、五版
19	25	20
20	21	21
21	22	2
22	23	23
23	26	24
24	27	24
25	29	24
26	66	24
27	30	24
28	31	24
29	32	24
30	33	24
31	34	24
32	35	24
33	37	24
34	38	24
35	39	24
36	40	24
37		
38	49	48
39	56	54
40	57	55
41	58	56
42	6	58
43	1	59

第一版	第二版	第三、四、五版
44	62	60
45		
46	73	68
47	45	42
48	46	43
49	74	69
50	75	70
51	76	71
52	78	72
53	79	73
54	81	75
55	82	76
56	83	77
57	87	80
58	88	81
59	89	82
60	94	87
61	91	84
62	92	85
63	93	86
64	95	88
65	96	89
66	97	90
67	98	91
68	100	92

第一版	第二版	第三、四、五版
69	101	93
70	102	94
71	103	95
72	104	96
73	108	99
74	109	100
75	110	101
	8	8
	14	
	20	第18首注
	28	
	36	33
	41	38
	42	39
	43	40
	44	
	47	46
	48	47
	50	49
	51	50
	52	51
	53	52
	54	53
	55	41
	59	57

第一版	第二版	第三、四、五版
	63	61
	62	64
	65	
	67	64
	68	65
	69	44
	70	45
	71	66
	72	67
	77	
	80	74
	84	78
	85	79
	86	
	90	83
	99	
	105	97
	10	98
	107	

总跋

文爱艺

奥马尔·哈亚姆于11世纪中叶出生于霍拉桑的内沙布尔（即今伊朗），在12世纪中前期去世。在奥马尔·哈亚姆的一生中，始终伴随着两位重要的人物，他们与他处在同一时代的同一国家，也正是其中一位讲述了这个有关他们三人爱恨情仇的故事。这便是尼扎姆·莫尔克（Nizám-ul-Mulk），曾任苏丹阿尔斯兰及其子马利克沙的宰相。他从穆罕默德的昏庸后人手中夺取了波斯地区并建立了塞尔柱王朝，最终激起欧洲人的十字军东征。

尼扎姆·莫尔克在遗言——或遗嘱中写下了这一切，将它作为留给未来政治家的记事录。以下内容是从历史学家米尔孔德发表于《加尔各答评论》第59期的文章《刺客史》中引用的。

“霍拉桑最伟大的智者之一就是内沙布尔的伊玛姆·穆瓦法克（Imám Mowaffak），这是一位德高望重的人——愿上帝祝福他的灵魂。他度过了85年的光辉岁月，当时人们普遍相信，每一个读过《古兰经》或是在伊玛姆的教导下研习过礼仪的少年，必定会获得荣耀和幸福。因此，我父亲把我从图斯送去内沙布尔，在法学博士伊玛姆门下学习，接受名师的指导。他总是用欣赏和善意的目光注视着我，而作为他的学生，我能时刻感受到他极大的热情和全身心的投入。就这样，我在他的教导下度过了 4 年的时光。在我初次来这里的时候，同时来了两个与我年纪相仿的新同学，这便是奥马尔·哈亚姆和命运多舛的哈桑·本·萨马赫。他们俩都有过人的智慧和极高的天分，我们三人就这样结成了挚友。每当伊玛姆暂停讲授抬起头来时，我们三个就复述刚刚听到的内容。奥马尔是内沙布尔本地人，而哈桑的父亲则是个阿里（Ali，什叶派信徒），是一个对生活和言行非常严谨的人，却囿于教义上的门户之见。一天，哈桑对我和哈亚姆说：‘伊玛姆的学生必将得到命运的垂青，这一点是众所周知的。就算我们现在都还一无所有，但无疑我们中至少会有一个人在将来拥有财富。我们何不为未来许下共同的承诺？’我们两个回答道：‘就按你说的做吧。’‘那好，’他说，‘我们就立下誓言，当财富降临到任何一人头上时，他皆要与他人平分而不得独享。’‘就那么办。’我俩回应道，并各自许下了承诺。岁月如梭，我从霍拉桑去往河中，又漫游到加兹尼和喀布尔。当我回国时，政府聘请了我，并在阿尔普·阿尔斯兰任苏丹期间升任宰相。

“他回国时已是多年以后，两个学生时代的老友终于找到了他，并要求按照学生时代立下的誓言分享他的财富。宰相非常慷慨地兑现了自己的诺言，就哈桑要求在政府里谋份差事，他向苏丹请示并满足了哈桑这个愿望。然而，因为对按部就班的升迁心怀不满，哈桑卷入一场政变阴谋。他本想借助阴谋取代恩人的位置，但最终在失败后遭到废黜并永不叙用。经过多年的不幸和流浪生活，哈桑成为伊斯玛仪派的首领。这本是一个长期潜伏、身份低微、活动于暗处的狂热教派，在他邪恶的欲望和野心的推动下，发展成了一个庞大的邪恶组织。1090年，在鲁德巴省，他控制了阿尔穆特的城堡，这座城堡坐落在里海南端沿线的山麓。这个被十字军称为“山中老人”的人物恶名昭著，他以这片山麓为根据地，在伊斯兰世界不断制造恐怖事件。由此产生了一个颇有争议的问题，即作为黑暗记忆遗留到现代欧洲语言中的单词‘杀手’，究竟源于何处。一种说法是它源于印度大麻，或是从中提取的鸦片，这些东西可以令人癫狂并让东方诸国陷入绝境；另一种说法是源自王朝创建者的名字，这个人的身影曾在内沙布尔的宁静校园里出现过，他就是死在这些杀手匕首下的无数受害者之一、三个朋友中的一个——尼扎姆·莫尔克。

“奥马尔·哈亚姆也去宰相那里要求分享自己的那份财富，却未要求一官半职。‘你可给予我的最大恩惠，’他说，‘就是让我在你财富庇护的一角安静地生活，去广泛传播科学的优异，且为你的健康和富足祈祷。'宰相对我们说，当他发现奥马尔是真正虔诚地做出这个决定时，便不再给他施压，只是从自己的财富中赐给了他一份1200密黄金的年金。

"奥马尔·哈亚姆就这样在内沙布尔定居，直到死去。'他忙于'——宰相补充道——'汲取各种各样的知识，特别是天文学方面，在这一领域，他取得了很高的成就。'在苏丹马利克沙的时代，他来到梅尔夫，因在科学方面的出色造诣而赢得了很高的赞誉，苏丹对他也甚为青睐。

"当苏丹马利克沙决定修改日历时，奥马尔便是八位被请去做这一工作的学者之一。成果便是贾拉利历（以苏丹全名中的一部分'贾拉尔·乌德·丁'来命名）——'一种时间计算方法'，吉本说，'它优于儒略历，其精确性接近于公历。'他同时也是一些天文图表的作者，后来被命名为'Zíji-Malikshåhí'在法国出版，他的一本关于代数的阿拉伯语论著也被翻译出版。

"他那带有诗意的姓氏哈亚姆（Khayyám），意为'帐篷制造者'，据说在莫尔克赠给他财产之前，他曾一度从事那方面的生意。许多波斯诗人的名字都源于他们所从事的职业，例如，阿塔尔，'一个药剂师'；阿萨尔，'一个榨油工'等。奥马尔在以下天马行空的诗句中，暗示了自己名字的意义：

哈亚姆，他曾缝制科学的帐篷，
如今落入痛苦的炉中，被深深地灼伤；
命运之刀砍断了他生存之篷的绳索，
希望这个骗子又将他出卖！

"我们只有一桩逸事来阐述他的生平，却是与他最息息相关的一桩。这桩逸事来源于他的诗集中的一篇匿名序言，有时同诗歌前言相混。在托马斯·海德著《古波斯宗教史》第529页的附录中，可以找到它的波斯语原文；德尔贝洛在《东方全书》的“希亚姆”（即哈亚姆）条目下也提及这桩逸事。

“这一切被写在古代编年史中，在伊斯兰教纪元517年（巴比伦纪元1123年），这位智者奥马尔·哈亚姆死于内沙布尔；在科学领域他是无与伦比的——是那个时代的典范。尼扎米，他的一位学生，讲述了下面的故事：‘我经常和我的老师奥马尔·哈亚姆在花园中交谈。有一天他对我说：‘北风会把花儿带来，覆盖我的墓地。’他的话令我惊奇，但我知道这绝非戏言，因为他从不说虚话。若干年后，我偶然重访内沙布尔，走到他的长眠之地。哦，看哪！他的墓地恰好在一个花园的外面，果树把结满累累果实的枝丫伸出墙来，把花撒满墓地，连墓碑也埋在落花之中。”

从《加尔各答评论》上引用的内容到此为止。据该文章的作者称，当他在印度读到这个关于奥马尔墓地的故事时，不禁联想起西塞罗曾经在记述中提到，阿基米德位于叙拉古的坟墓就埋没在百草之中。我记得托尔瓦德森也曾希望自己的坟墓上开满玫瑰。我相信，这一虔诚的愿望在今日一定会得以满足。下面，我们还是回到奥马尔身上。

虽然苏丹对奥马尔表现出了欣赏之情，但是奥马尔的大胆思想和言辞使得人们认为，他藐视所处的时代和国家。据说苏菲教徒对他甚为憎恨，他毫不掩饰自己对神秘主义和伊斯兰教的嘲讽，认为苏菲教派的践行荒谬，信条不值一提。他们的诗人，包括伊斯兰教徒哈菲兹（菲尔多西除外）在波斯颇受尊崇，也广泛地借用了奥马尔诗歌作为素材，只是将它转化为神秘主义的形式，更贴近于他们自身及其诗歌所及的人。这群人对信仰和怀疑颇为敏感，对肉体感官和精神意识同样敏锐；他们借助诗歌的翅膀自由地游走于天堂和人间、今生与来世，并对此颇为享受。奥马尔十分忠诚于自己的心灵和思想。他相信命运而非天意，追随今生而非来世，并试图将它们发挥到极致。他宁愿借助于眼睛所看到的事物将感性的灵魂归为平静，而不是徒劳地困惑于它们本身的样子。由此可知，他对世界的野心并不大，他更倾向于让感性凌驾于智性之上，从幽默和邪僻的欢愉中得到自我满足、获得欢乐。虽然这让他与大多数人一样，总是不能为自己的问题找到答案，即使这些问题对他来说是至关重要的。

无论出自何种原因，如前所说，奥马尔在自己的国家从未受到欢迎，因此被卑劣地遣送国外。他的诗歌手稿的破损程度高于一般东方论著手稿的平均损坏度，因而在东方极为稀少，能够逃过军事和科学的扫荡而流往西方的就更罕见了。印度政府没有副本，巴黎国家图书馆也没有。我们所知的只是一个在英格兰的副本：牛津大学图书馆，乌斯利第140号印本，1460年写于舍拉兹。这个本子包括了《柔波集》158首。另一个在加尔各答的亚洲协会图书馆，包括了516首，虽然已通过收集各种副本和片段集增加了不少诗歌，但仍不是全部。冯·汉默说他的复制本包括大约200首，但是斯普林格博士经过检索之后，觉得这个数字值得怀疑。在牛津大学和加尔各答图书馆的这些副本，好像是以一种抗议的方式写成的，每一个都以一首四行诗作为开头（不论是否写得有天分），以英文字母为序。牛津本以一个道歉开始；加尔各答本是一篇谏言，假设（一个副本的序言如此写）诗人从梦中苏醒，在梦里奥马尔的母亲在祈问他将来的命运，便以这样的方式呈现：

哦，心内如焚，为了这些在燃烧的人，
在地狱里，这些火焰就会转而扑向你，
哭泣的时间有多长，“对他们降下仁慈吧，上帝”！

为什么，你不教导它以艺术，而他来学？

伯德雷恩的四行诗向神恳求公正：

如果我自己疏于神的信条
散乱了美好品行的串珠，
就让这成为我唯一恳求的罪赎，
我从此不会误读其中一二。

从书评人那里我知悉了奥马尔传奇的一生，包括他将奥马尔和卢克莱修作为具有自然品行和超然天分的诗人相比较所做的论述。两人都拥有敏感、强健、过人的智慧、出色的想象力，以及坚持真理和正义的内心。他们秉持公正，反叛自己国家的伪宗教以及对其错误和愚蠢的献身。他们怀着美好的愿望推翻这一切，却因缺乏更好的启发来引导他们，因而无法找到替代物，也无法建立相关的法律。实际上，卢克莱修以伊壁鸠鲁提供的材料作为依据，满足于自己的“大机器随机偶然建造理论”，将自己的行动依从于一个无法律可依的准则，成为一个较为坚忍的人，但他还不是一个严格的伊壁鸠鲁式人物。他端坐凝思，在对罗马戏剧的高妙叙说中，观看自己也是其中一个角色的宇宙机器大戏，而悬浮在观众和太阳之间的垂幕所散发的惊人反射，也使得关于他的一切变得暗淡下来。奥马尔对于这种复杂的体系更不抱希望和毫不在乎，这种体系只会引向绝望的必然性。伴随着苦涩和幽默的嘲弄，他将自己的天赋和学识恣意抛向毁灭。他将假装感官欢愉作为生命的真正目的，并用那些抽象的问题来自娱自乐，例如神性、命运、物质和精神、善与恶；他也乐于自困于所谓的人生追求。而所有的一切到最后都沦落为异常令人疲倦的闹剧！

按照当前的译本，最初的《柔波集》（阿拉伯语无喉音，这些四行诗朗读起来更富有音乐性）包含的是独立诗节，平均有四行，韵律各异，有时全部押韵，有些像是希腊的四行诗，倒数第二节好像是在抬高或是悬置，音调在最后一行落下，神似我国古老的《绝句》。

《柔波集》如通常的东方诗歌体一样，依从字母韵——一种严肃、华丽而奇怪的连续性。在这里所选取的是一串牧歌式的诗歌，一小部分的“饮酒作乐”歌，在原本中（无论是否为真迹）一再重现。

无论所取道路如何，结果总是那么悲伤：最悲伤的或许是当所有浮华过尽，悲伤将比愤怒更容易逼近这个制帐篷的老人。他倾尽所有却仍无法摆脱命运的镣铐，对未来也只能投去无望的一瞥，最后跌回眼前的尘世。

明日何其多，他却只能孤立于今朝，看着时光瞬间从脚下滑落。

文爱艺，当代著名作家、诗人、翻译家，中国作家协会会员。生于湖北省襄阳市，从小精读古典诗词，十四岁开始发表作品。

著有《春祭》《梦裙》（2版）、《夜夜秋雨》（2版）、《太阳花》（9版）、《寂寞花》（4版）、《雨中花》（2001－2002）、《病玫瑰》（2003－2004）、《温柔》《独坐爱情之外》《梦的岸边》《流逝在花朵里的记忆》《生命的花朵》《长满翅膀的月亮》《伴月星》《一帘梦》《雪花的心情》《来不及摇醒的美丽》《成群结队的梦》《我的灵魂是火焰•文爱艺抒情诗选集》（1976－2000）、《像心一样敞开的花朵•文爱艺散文诗选集》（1976－2000）、《玫瑰花园》《文爱艺诗歌精品赏析集》（全三卷）、《文爱艺抒情诗集（全三册）——追逐彩蝶•断桥边的红莲•白雪唤醒的纯洁•典藏本赏析版》《文爱艺抒情诗集》《文爱艺散文诗集》《文爱艺爱情诗集》（12版•插图本）、《文爱艺诗集》（12版•插图本）、《文爱艺诗集•第62部•夜歌》《文爱艺诗集•第63部•彼岸花》《文爱艺诗集•第64部•青春》《文爱艺全集》（诗1－4卷•数字版）等60多部诗集，深受读者喜爱，再版不断。

部分作品被译成英、法、俄、日、阿拉伯、世界语等文。现主要致力于系列小说的创作。

译有《勃朗宁夫人十四行爱情诗集》（插图本）、《亚当夏娃日记》（10版•插图本）、《柔波集》（2版•插图本）、《恶之花》（13版•全译本•赏析版•插图本）、《风中之心》《奢侈品之战》《沉思录》（8版•插图本）、《箴言录》（8版•插图本）、《思想录》（插图本）、《古埃及亡灵书》（2版•灵魂之书•插图本）、《小王子》（5版•插图本）、《一个孩子的诗园》（9版•插图本）、《天真之歌》（插图本）、《经验之歌》（插图本）、《亚瑟王传奇》（2版•插图本）、《墓畔挽歌》（2版•插图本）、《老人与海》（3版•插图本）、《培根随笔全集》《共产党宣言》等经典名著及其他著作。

编著有《离骚》《天问》《九歌》《九章》《九辩》《兰亭集》（2版•插图本）《绝句》《花之魂》《中国古代风俗百图》（2版•插图本）《道德经》《金刚经》《心经》《茶经》《酒经》《草书／元•鲜于枢书唐诗》《行书／宋•米芾书天马赋》《诗二十四品》《孟浩然全集》《陈子昂全集》《中国时间》《中国病人》《静心录》《净心录》《洗冤集录》《经典书库》《新诗金库》《品质书库》《品质诗库》等书。

另出版有《当代寓言大观》（4卷）、《当代寓言名家名作》（9卷）、《当代寓言金库》（10卷）、《开启儿童智慧的100个当代寓言故事》等少儿读物。

所著、译、编图书，连获2015年（首届）、2016年、2018年“海峡两岸十大最美图书”奖，11部获2011年、2012年、2013年、2015年、2016年、2017年、2018年，“中国最美图书”奖；《文爱艺爱情诗集》（第9版）获2019年环球设计大奖视觉传达类金奖，《文爱艺爱情诗集》（第10版）获2017年台湾金点大奖、2018年美国NY TDC 64 TDC Communication Design Winners大奖，《文爱艺爱情诗集》（第12版）再获香港2018年HKDA环球设计大奖GDA银奖；《文爱艺诗集•第62部•夜歌》获铜奖，且再获美国2018年ONE SHOW DESIGN 优异奖、2019年第六十五届美国Certificate of Typographic Excellence年度优异奖。

《文爱艺诗集》获“世界最美图书”奖。

图书在版编目（CIP）数据

柔波集 ： 集校版全集 / (波斯) 奥马尔·哈亚姆著；(英) 爱德华·菲茨杰拉德，文爱艺译. -- 北京 ： 北京航空航天大学出版社，2019.10

ISBN 978-7-5124-2997-0

Ⅰ. ①柔… Ⅱ. ①奥… ②爱… ③文… Ⅲ. ①诗集－伊朗－中世纪 Ⅳ. ①I373.23

中国版本图书馆CIP数据核字(2019)第076723号

柔波集：集校版全集

[波斯] 奥马尔·哈亚姆 著
[英] 爱德华·菲茨杰拉德 英译
文爱艺 译

出版统筹：邓永标
责任编辑：曲建文 舒 心
责任印制：马文敏
书籍设计：胡 茬
策划制作：爱艺书院 美书坊 郭艺媛
出版发行：北京航空航天大学出版社
地址：北京市海淀区学院路 37 号（100191）
电话：(010)82317023（编辑部） (010)82317024（发行部） (010)82316936（邮购部）
网址：www.buaapress.com.cn
读者信箱：bhxszx@163.com
印刷：鑫艺佳利（天津）印刷有限公司
开本：787mm×1092mm 1/16
印张：25.5
字数：202千字
版次：2019 年 10 月第 1 版
印次：2019 年 10 月第 1 次印刷
书号：ISBN 978-7-5124-2997-0
定价：368.00 元
